Bubble Entendre

Bubble Entendre

Mark Waugh

Semina No. 3

Untitled (Paper, ink)

Name Dropping

The hooded station of St Pancras let trains come and go on glistening rails. I arrived from Paris with a small bag. I hurried through the dense platforms towards the underground. It was hot and the proliferation of bodies was enticing. You could lick and collude with the heat and breathe in the dream of endless pleasures. I put the catastrophe of global warming and my economic meltdown on ice. I was making a deal. The thought made me smile despite the crush of the tube. This was worse than I remembered. It was an Olympic crush. The infrastructure was ill-equipped for the population of the city in 2012.

The summer evening stretched across the city from the red brickwork of the British Library to the abandoned yellow safety helmets that circled the Olympic Stadium.

Among the shoddy seats and corporate booze, eighty thousand people were joined by zillions worldwide. This was history as media stampede; 'content' distribution on every type of mashed-up and pimped-out piece of techno shit. The focus of a transcendental silence was the abdominal muscles of a Nike-clad star of the women's 1,500m race and the sound to come. The fatal crack from the starting pistol. Seconds break down into milliseconds. The heartbeat rises a few bpm. Athletes and the stadium audience drip in concentration. Bodies lined up for the spectacle of classical serial orgasms. London ready to roar.

In the city there is no resistance to information; we are punctured by data and promulgate our knowledge through indifference to the spectacle. Bang. We jump…

The security around the stadium was awesome. Between east and west London historic cultural divides played themselves out. In Mayfair the police were not prepared for trouble. In Claridge's, oblivious to the track events, new medal holders were milking their moment. Ghosts of Victorian prizefighters dragged west with knuckles raw and bloodied to clasp drafts of intoxication. The public bars were heaving and the suites stank of money. Two gorgeous gymnasts were among my guests in room 212. I had taken it in folly. I wanted to be close to White City for a morning meeting with Becky and the daft director who was lined up to shoot *Amour de Post*, my biography of Madame de Sévigné. I'd wanted room 568 but it was taken. I'd booked online between Vitre and Paris.

'I owe you the true story!', I declared, stumbling out of the Art Deco wreckage naked beside Kim. Two humiliated captives suddenly and unexpectedly alive and free.

Our story was known all around the world. We were stars. The curator Simon, the actress Becky, the author, myself, athletes Kim and Quim, plus the Tory MP Tim.

The minute-by-minute ordeal was relayed online by our hosts. They forced us to strip off and get into bed. Meanwhile terrestrial TV showed archive footage of us before we were hostages with voice-over speculation about the identity of the terrorists. The world waited for the next episode between clips of athletes standing on podiums.

My agent had negotiated deals out of desperation rather than avarice. It was all she could do. The photo shoot was worth more than the annual returns of *The Jissom Snake*, my last novel. And I was running late.

'Can you turn the umbrella this way a little?', asked a girl dressed in functional apparel.

The entourage of make-up assistants and psychic fluffers are ready and waiting for William Shakespeare to arrive at the hotel.

The novel would be ready in days. Lottie, bless her, had arranged a small team of crack lexicographers to work collaboratively with me and the transcripts from the siege. Thank God, as it was still a bit of a daze to me.

It was to be edited and typeset in a modest but refined font. Lottie knew the designer, who specialised in monographs by contemporary artists but could do wonders with unruly pagination. She gave him the working title—*Mayfair Memoir*. An ironic choice playing on my nakedness and hostage romance. A few phrases here and there might retain my decadent cadence, a lubricated animosity stalking the periphery of the story. I discovered on my first call as a free man that we had sold separate audio rights and various names were being dropped as contenders for my role.

I fretted it might sound too cool on morning TV and those myriad mobile channels that service the City. It would do me no harm with the BBC or the deal on my fairy tales from the court of Versailles.

'What reading are you getting now?', the photographer asked.

Vogue had booked an early shoot and specified a set-up in an east London suite. It was vast with light coming in from a long window. It framed the Gherkin perfectly. The bedroom had a walk-in closet and en suite bathroom. It was bigger than my siege suite. This detail was so comforting, so normal, I felt as if I had stepped through the mirror into the afterlife, a post-mortal culture.

Becoming famous overnight requires watching the execution of your former self. After three days of debriefing and two days of freedom I had learned a lot. Well, two points are worth communicating while I am sober.

Firstly I discovered my old books were hot. Fans were editing a supplementary oeuvre online. I bookmarked a site called *Mnemonic Fetishes*. On it I found this extract from *Come*.

'…[h]ymen debris and other flowers of rhetoric. Fort (distance) Da(return). I used to play with girls, words, writing machines and artefacts of flight…but now? Her plasticity amazes me. My dreaming solitudinal voice-over tries to make sense of senseless things, the grotesque hallucination of corroding missiles falling like confetti from another story. A story far from here. This decimal neurosis bleeds into the fiction. A sentence is marooned in the story. Reading is painfully slow. I want to be at a strip show of the unconscious revealing the lewd artifice of the naked truth. Thus I put on

the aura of DS and hide myself behind her moulded nipples.
Through her semi-opaque body I peep like…'

Another thing I realised after I became prime-time news was
that I had no sense of time.

The traffic stalled. I was trapped in a cab on a London street
and it was bliss. I didn't care how late I was. The relief my
appearance would release in those awaiting me could only
add to the glamour of my arrival. This story would be hailed as
my most intimate achievement. No interlocutors or fabrications
of subjectivity. The audience knew all my flaws and…after
all the full stops, eclipsed ellipses of *Bubble Entendre…*this
was it, lights, camera and everything!

It meant writing in an assumed voice of course. I thought of
my old friend Maurice. He was perfect for this part. I'm too shy
to act out, even on the silent page. Lottie set the ghouls a few
formal rules. These were with regards to the regularity of the
sex 'n' drug references, and a few idiosyncrasies of punctuation.

The ghouls were discreet about their trade and my traits.
Not even their closest friends knew the novels they sutured.
While I walked around a graveyard in Ripe, Lottie paid off
their vanity with cash and the offer of time on the French job,
if it came off.

I was nothing, just flesh in a room waiting to die. Waiting for the
girl in the red plastic jacket and custom Vans to blow me away.

The question mark over sales ripped open like a stuffed elephant
in the gas-filled hotel room. The SAS broke in with their

Paris Vision cameras focused on my flesh. Viewers might have thought I was screeching, 'Once upon a Time', but I only dreamt it and so this is not how the story starts. Now it just begins with a crack. And POW!!!

Store in a Cool Place

I used to like cross-country running because it provided opportunities to smoke and get drunk during sports. Iris thought running ran in the family but I know it's an English tradition. Only fools pretend that sport is an end in itself. It is, and always has been, a means to an end. The aim is to reduce culture to a spectacle of bestial performance.

It is ironic that I became the story that fucked up the Olympics. It was fun to be the centre of attention. My old life was over but I had given sport a run for its money.

I became a switching screen for all the schizophrenic staging posts of belief. I was all the Gods and their acolytes from Mars through Zeus. And an infinity of other names too. And in this way I imprisoned them, for that was the will of the City—the logic after Ur—to be done with God and his false prophets of control. In that magic moment I reached the limits of my calling.

'I am reality at twenty-four frames per second—nothing more—no thing!'

'I am a Model—a no thing?'

I wrote this down with the precision of a fatal biological strategy. It was a lucid delusion. I had made it to the hotel

but was late and sweating. Some things don't change. I saw
the double digits in red glowing text.

'Weren't you in the *News of the World*?'

Then the cabbie stopped the meter and chirped, 'That'll be
twenty-five fifty mate.'

Porn Free

Shakespeare woke up on the second day of freedom with
a cock like a crowbar and a vague memory. Between the siege
and years of languishing in front of the TV he had little reality
left to call his own. It was all out there. A consciousness
evacuated, his body in ruins.

He made his way to the en suite. In the bathroom mirror he fell
like Narcissus into the morbid pool of reflection.

Between the surfaces he recalled a glass-fronted penthouse
overlooking the Thames. On the walls were works from the
early *frieze* era. Sexy pieces by Marlene Dumas on paper,
an aluminum mounted, black and white cat in the snow by
Nobuyoshi Araki, a Julian Opie animated striptease, a girl
crouching on a chair and looking listlessly out of the frame
by Julia and a chic panel by Gary Hume of his ex-lover. Gazing
lovingly into the mirror, Shakespeare pondered the possibility
he was suffering from false memory syndrome.

Lucy and Memet are in a medieval lane behind St Paul's, breaking
the office rules. She lifts up her short tennis dress and vaults onto
his pole. She told him in the staff canteen that she could ride him

like a helicopter. She scribbled this on a napkin and spun it across the table in front of workers from another department.

While others wasted time on circulating agendas, refining organograms and checking their Facebook applications, he sent her texts. These vibrated softly in her pocket.

'If you run you're dead…if you stay, you're dead again', she observed.

They had found a niche and an air conditioning unit blew her hair as she hummed *Love in an Elevator*. He could only hear the spinning of the fan. Feeling his frantic acceleration she pulled his cock from her cunt and turned to face him. Further east the runners were half a mile into the race. She got him to sit on a green bin and pulled her dress back down. He pulled out his mobile and focused the eight megapixel camera.

Her hair was still blowing in the wind as she pulled off the protection and spat on his cock. She looked deep into his eyes. She had lost control and didn't give a fuck if anyone saw her. Lucy jerked Memet's cock into her mouth and rubbed herself. She felt her wet crack give a little and her clitoris jump. Sucking cock was the only way she could climax.

Lucy looked up at Memet and licked the tip of his prick collecting beads of sticky dew. Then she took his cock deep into her throat again. It descended like an escalator diving towards the Piccadilly Line. His hand cradled her head as she worked herself to orgasm and moaned. Memet pulled back and tried to keep her framed as he shot his milk over her face.

The papers said it was from China via Turkey that the stimulants had travelled to London. The papers called them techno-drugs. Rumours circulated before the games. An ancient trade route but a new traffic. Xenophobia as old as the Book itself? The drug carried by the two sixteen-year-old gymnasts was third-generation nanopharmocology. It gave them a point five twist on their rivals and tantric powers of deferred climax.

Or so Kim said on the third day of freedom.

It was an arousing call. She dexterously recounted the pleasure she took in rough sex. She liked sex to be dirty and impulsive. Sex was playing possession and possessed. Letting her body bruise and bruising another's flesh. A physical assault on the cerebral apathy of the body. Wrenching flesh into extreme physical states. It was what they were trained to do. Dropping down hard on the bar, throwing her body on the floor, stretching fragile architectures to breaking point. She could do handstands, crabs, suspend her body indefinitely, mock the limits of physical exhaustion.

I listened to her strongly accented English. I kept my ear close to the phone until it was hot and sweat dripped down my neck. Inside her phonetic painting Shakespeare vapourised, becoming a satyr's breath in her wet dream. Her dishevelled figure a trap for Quim's javelin. Her moat of lilies a fatal depth. His tip a searing quarry in her wound. And when she came it was the scream of the stadium muted by pillows.

Norwegian Wood

Post-*Vogue* interviews had been arranged with gossip magazines and less prestigious titles. I said yes to everything.

Fame was so intoxicating. I secured a room at the Citadel of Satan on Dean Street, known to some as The Groucho. You might have thought experience would put me off hotels but I am vulnerable to their monastic simplicity. I also found old habits die hard. I like the free soap and shower gel.

I was suffering from post-siege trauma. During the Beijing Olympics I hooked up with a cultural delegation from the UK. I stayed in The Red Capital Hotel. It was a shrine to Chairman Mao. A perfect place to bring guests after the games.

At that time I was casting myself as Todger from Dickens. I sat on Dean Street and imagined I could recite a line of two of Victorian prose to Kim.

'She touched his organ, and from that bright epoch even it, the old companion of his happiest hours, incapable as he had thought of elevation, began a new and deified existence.'

Kim and I had shared trauma but that is nothing. I should have sat down like Madame de Sévigné and composed a detailed emotional account. I should have let her go quietly to her Beijing high-rise, gazing out over erased memories. But she was still in London and long emails are a drag.

I speed-dialled Lottie. Our conversation was not good. She thought a woodcut by the Norwegian artist Edward Munch, and in particular *The Vampire*, was wrong for the cover.

Lottie had inherited a publishing house. Some inherit titles, debts, or pets…Lottie had been dumped with an upmarket brand. She rode out the demise of the independents by diversifying into print on demand, iStory, and complicated derivative intellectual property rights. She was sharp, efficient and not at leisure to listen to listless and untaught ideas about Norwegian woodcuts, Dickens, wet rooms, seduction, trauma or fidelity. However, mine was a felicitous break for the company as she had a new series of arty titles to promote and PR is never cheap.

I am William Shakespeare. They might have heard of me. Worse still you might have read me. I don't like to précis my works. I am always depressed by the sentence that starts 'I am…'

I was not a storyteller. I was filling every second with narrative, insane plots, conspiracies about our hosts, and the drugs in Kim and Quim.

I was in my room imagining all the fun happening below in the bar. I fantasised about sitting with Kim and introducing her to Michael and the decadent spectres down the street in The Colony Rooms which was next door. Lottie told me her aunt hung out there in the 1960s. It is alleged that a Francis Bacon painting of this aunt's hands adorned the emerald green walls for years.

2012 Mixed Media

The story would be from one of his early novels. *Come* perhaps or *Bubble Entendre*, but not *The Jissom Snake*. The Mayan cosmology and the back streets of a medieval French town would create background ambience. They were rich and famous after all, and you don't get anywhere without carving out a narrative of sorts, or accruing a few intriguing details.

He realised if they got out they would be picked off by the PR militia. Who encouraged Madame de Sévigné or her daughter to publish their intimate archive? His mind was wondering. He was no closer to starting his performance. The games. The world. The terror. The perfected media loops of communication. This telepathic accuracy. Inside the mind of the 'terror cell'. Inside the retina of the hostage. Inside the hallucination that was the ending of the world in 2012 in room 212.

'Knowledge is a drug, the ear an open vein!'

Outside on the pavement around Claridge's the police were hastily coordinating their actions. In his imagination the SAS were scanning the fabric of the building assuming the positions needed to make an assault. He knew these would be calculated regardless of the threat of execution offered by the hosts.

'It hasn't changed much since I was here for Jago's last birthday party. Albi was a baby and little Ruby and Violet danced to the orchestra until Bianca swirled them around beneath the crystal chandeliers. Roc and I sat with Jequetta and Dan sipping Earl Grey tea, savouring the neat oblong sandwiches…Oh, and waiters came with the tea and left the pot on the mantelpiece…'

It was the image of his friend dead that he saw in that instant and only for a fraction of a second. Then he saw his godchildren on the black carriage singing, *The Grand Old Duke of York* as the funeral procession moved towards the church up the winding path from Port Eliot. Then nothingness came back like an incorrigible puppy and he was elsewhere. We are never where we want to be except in orgasm. And then we are so abstract we don't know where we are.

الـمخـدرهي الـمعرفـه

Like the Mayans I calculated the finitude of attention and
the limits of the universe. That is one thing we must say about
the 'terror'. It made us notice the pleasure of nothingness.
The bomb was cruel without doubt and I had done nothing
to provoke it. But it wasn't torture. Perhaps a bullet but not
sadistic lingering pleasure. I didn't think that was on the menu
at Claridge's despite the t-shirts that read, *Burn Baby Burn
Kernow Inferno!*

Some wag at the *Guardian* would say that these were surrealists
not terrorists who claimed random crimes as their own. Since
the defeat of An Gof in 1497 at the battle of Deptford Bridge
regular waves of Cornish radicals had demanded freedom from
occupation. In 2007, more than 500 years after the massacre,
the Cornish National Liberation Army was reported as making
threats via an Arab based server. I really had no idea what this
mob of surfers were after—maybe a place in the Olympics?
I wondered if they had seen the writing on the wall in Bond
Street which read *Five Forced to Romp in Naked Orgy.*

Give Peace a Chance

I don't need to elaborate on the fact that Yoko Ono was
a Japanese performance artist. Like her contemporary Yayoi
Kusama she emerged in the 1960s as a new voice of the Japanese
aesthetic. Like the Bread Man, she was an early member of
Fluxus in New York. Conceptual, playful and happy to get
naked if it provoked an audience, for example in *Cut Piece*.
In her most famous work *Bed*, she lay in bed with John Lennon
in room 702 of the Amsterdam Hilton.

She knew their marriage would be a massive media event
and suggested they stage a protest against the war in Vietnam.
As the archives show, they lay in bed and invited the world into
their suite decorated with A4 sheets of paper that read 'Peace'
and 'Love'. After being told to strip I immediately thought
of John and Yoko in bed in 1969.

I went to Beijing to cover the last Olympics. I had followed
the Olympic torch on TV and was curious about who would
turn up in the warm smog of Beijing.

They called early one morning. I was on the train and almost
missed the call. They offered me a decent fee and expenses.
Spielberg had walked away like Schindler into an ethical silence.
Maybe someone told them that I saw the Olympic preparations
in Beijing in 2004. The nest rising out of the fog. The cranes
towering over the old Houdongs, the lone red lantern hanging
in the gateway of the home that has disappeared.

A delicate girl who metamorphosed into an explosion of
biodynamic volition. Sweet Kim and her pop CDs bought in the
new Soho. Her golden slippers racing beyond the Argonauts,
past Cinderella and into a future that arrives as she sleeps,
coiled on the seat of the long flight home. She is undisturbed
by turbulence or the replay of her victory on the screens
around her.

In the Forbidden City the face of Mao smiles on the people. Like
Walt Disney he sleeps on ice, guarded by an endless and solemn
procession of visitors. The storm broke as I passed around
the back of Tiananmen Square. I rushed past tourists buying
exquisite gourd pipes, huddled into the jumble of boxes, bikes
and guitars. Music played as the rain fell. This was the shop
owned by Kim's parents. The profit helped with her training.

The street became a river and all around chaos was surging. The locals stood under the eves of the stores watching the frantic search for taxis and routes out of the centre of the city.

'When would the rain stop?', I asked. A shrug, a laugh, no one knew. The immediacy of the storm, the fabric of the city shimmering in silver tributaries. Plastic bags as hats and shoes. From every overhang a waterfall fell.

Time is Out of Joint

The following day the sky over Beijing was Prussian blue. With my aquatinted memories I got the concierge to write down the address of the Lama Temple. I took a fast-moving taxi through roads crammed with cars and bikes that were already in the minority. At the temple beauty slowed the pace of visitors to a Zen-like stillness.

Only the occasional flash of a camera awoke the crowd from its reverie. Incense smoke wrapped itself around pomegranate trees and into the blue sky. What a difference some rain makes. It was good for the athletes too.

A convoy of taxis journeyed into the humid night air. The streets rocked to the beat of hybrid pop. International flags draped over bodies. We drove deep into the periphery down pot-holed roads and arrived at a gated house. There was a party inside. I met journalists, curators and artists, who had come as part of the delegation of the 2012 Cultural Olympiad.

My lips were soaked in mosquito repellent and I smoked a cigarette. Our drivers waited patiently, smoking and chatting in the distance. Their rates were by the mile rather than the minute. We left after ten minutes on another dash through the neon night.

Our destination was the huge factory complex of DZ 798. Here the stars of the Chinese art scene had their galleries and studios. This was where the international art market had established a cultural foothold in China's consciousness.

The hotel welcomed our return with endless smiles glazed across the faces of the hotel receptionists who wore smart pink suits. They stood posed beneath clocks that told the time across continental meridians. The hands of the clocks moved around the faces like runners in separate lanes, all heading in the same direction but advancing at different speeds.

This is My Story

Behind a mask of gaffer tape and feathers she leaned back and smiled. The man of letters was at her mercy and she made a simple request.

'Write me a story.'

'Sure', he said. The Hotel Monaco was a yes space. Everything and anything was possible there.

'Anything special you want me to write?'

'No, but I must be able to live it.'

'What, become a character, how would that work?'

'I don't know. You are the writer!'

'But the agency of a character in a novel transforms the reality of the narrative; you would change reality in a different world. The real world?'

'Well perhaps this novel would just be a series of rules.'

'But then it would not be a novel?'

'The limits of the novel are open to question.'

'I want a novel that starts in a hotel room in 2012.'

'Did that idea just pop into your head or is that something you dreamt up earlier?'

'I am not spontaneous.'

We are playing a serious game pretending to be hostages. We come after Munich and the Balcombe Street Siege. We are trapped in the confines of a hotel room and our broken flesh is disseminated on the screen of mediation.

On the screen the image is more chaotic. A black dude. Two white boys in front. The dude does it doggy style and the white boys wear Venetian masks and get blow jobs. It is a DIY version of *Eyes Wide Shut*. They switch positions. It is like a work by Vanessa Beecroft, a violent architecture of melamine scales. The girl lets her hair fall over her face. On the parquet floor lie articles of clothes she might have worn…She works hard to keep the head of a prick visible as the jissom shoots. It must feel good to have her suck you.

Mrs Robinson: I'll be up in five minutes.

Benjamin: Well, goodbye then.

Mrs Robinson: Benjamin.

Benjamin: Yes?

Mrs Robinson: Isn't there something you want to tell me?

Benjamin: Tell you?

Mrs Robinson: Yes.

Benjamin: Well, I want you to know how much
                 I appreciate this. Really!

Mrs Robinson: The number?

Benjamin: What?

Mrs Robinson: The room number, Benjamin. I think you
                 ought to tell me that.

Benjamin: Oh? You're absolutely right. Absolutely.
                 It's 568.

Berlin

Would I land a role in *Siegeworks no.3*, a work of art for
several bodies played by members of public? I had heard
of interventions and shots fired by artists at distant planes.
I thought the calls from hijacked planes had a terrible poetic

resonance with the powerlessness of the silent majority. In the anxiety of the spectacle of genocide they had fabricated the rules of the performance. It would be a global artwork. A relational experience bound together through the feedback of the media.

'Is a model of a bomb in a gallery a work of art or terror?'

His girlfriend was not in the room when the surfers stormed in wearing their colour-coded tracksuits.

A knife, a fork, a bottle and a cork, that's the way we spell New York.

Paris

SEX and the return to the city of *Come*. No. Yes. No. Yes. Another sofa. It is brown with paisley prints all over it. Another girl is slapping her pussy while a skinny chalky cock fucks her. She is looking down onto the camera and a dude is standing on the sofa and getting her to suck his balls and then take his charcoal stick in her mouth. The charcoal and chalk change positions. The chalk spurts his milkshake over her face. She keeps the cock in her mouth like a dummy as she moans. The charcoal stick spurts its load. She pleads, 'Yes…yes…yes… come in my face.' She blows little bubbles and spits it across her tits as she grins to the camera.

In the back of the taxi heading across town and losing all sense of urgency I began to think about this pressure to narrate what

had happened. To contain the experience. Write a scar
around the emotional details and stick to that coagulating
line. No erasures of over-writing. No layering of details.
It was important to know what I thought of the experience.

London

I am rarely able to remember anything after drinking. They
forced me to empty the minibar. We were not random hostages
but strategic targets. I mixed the tonics with the vodka and
gin. The coke went down with the scotch and then red wine
with white. I must have been drunk when they ordered me
to remove my clothes and Kim's too.

Kim was fit and as Adam Ant said 'ridicule is nothing to
be scared of'. I stripped down to my Boss underwear and then
paused. In the twisted perversity of my pimped-out psyche
I might have thought this will look daft on YouTube but might
lighten things up.

They didn't intend to kill Quim but he scared them when
he lunged at one of the surfers with a fork. I don't remember
what happened next. I'm told Kim screamed, and I did too.

Why was I still online on 26 July 2012?

The Path of the True Story

The prisoners were not at liberty to use the complimentary
Wi-Fi in the rooms. Through iChat they were making the siege

the medium of their protest. At first it went well. A militant love-in. But prisoners are not numbers and Kim was not playing *You-porn4peace*.

We just watched as they dragged Quim out of the room and into the en suite. The walls were left splattered with his blood.

We had the look of a neo-naturist lock-in. The hostages were not speaking.

A couple of girls sucking and humping some beefcake with a stiffy on the hotel TV porn channel.

Fairy tales.

Nord Ost

In a small gallery, wrapped in a silk daydress, another busy subject is glued to her mobile. Her head tilts as if trying to look at a canvas from a specific angle but maybe it's just the way she responds to the phone. In the office the meeting ends.

Multiple cuts to the face of the author and the other celebrities. They are all featured in a special 'Timeless Summer' issue of *CHILL*, on sale now. Seeing himself on the TV is disturbing. The footage reminded him of watching the Moscow Theatre siege. It had looked like a Bond film.

The man in the yellow tracksuit flips over to the porn channel and goes back and forth for a minute. Three guys in an alley with a girl doing gym poses. They wear rough jeans and Adidas sports tops. Their cocks are hard.

If he wanted reality he would force himself to watch re-runs
of ejaculations. Twins kissing and sucking as cocks splatter them
with ice cream. Or he could take in the beach furniture in Brazil
while not watching local home-grown action.

The porn made Kim and Becky nervous. They felt they were
going to have to perform. Why else were they naked with
these maniacs?

If they had read De Sade or Mister Trippy, they would be
indexing the thanatoerotic possibilities of the scene. As the artist
Fiona Banner had revealed in her subtle canvases of the 1990s,
there is a lot of surface detail in porn.

They came to die on a wet evening, a romance, *Nord Ost* set
in Stalin's Russia. They came in at the interval. The theatre
audience heard nothing as machine guns sprayed the auditorium.
On the video recording of the show, the Brechtian fourth wall
collapsed and in a classic putsch, terrorists took the stage in
place of the actors. A hostage called out to the local radio station.
If the demands were not met the theatre would be blown up
and the audience sent to kingdom come with it.

The furnishings of Claridge's were too tasteful for a porn
shoot. With all of that lush fake Art Deco you couldn't stage
good wood there. Not even *Nice Bahira*.

Outside the police had sealed off the streets. No tube trains
at Bond Street station. The musical *42nd Street* was another
potential target. The women wore their bomb belts like
still-born babies. The dead in the room with the living.
The living and the soon-to-be-dead make eye contact.

They shot three bullets into her. That was two days into the siege. They had real guns and our hopes of getting out were dying.

The Moscow Theatre finally emptied out. Theatre died another death. The hostages died in their seats.

He had stopped looking at his watch but the TV reminded him of how interminable the ordeal was. It could go on for weeks.

Shaven and Scanned

We all know what demands the terrorists will make.
We are easily distracted by the pleasures of confined spaces.
They are siege artists and the medium is democratic.

A phone rings. A woman in her early thirties with longish blond hair answers it. Her manner is curt. Like she doesn't watch hot DIY sex and wouldn't want to. She gently spins the chair around in a yes-no, yes-no manner. Her desk is littered with envelopes, papers, photographs, make-up. If she had sex it would be with the scanner and shelves all around her. Her castle of office ephemera.

Spinning chairs are of course great office sex aides. They bring a giddy pleasure to the most routine on-the-job straight to web cam action.

The man in the yellow tracksuit was called out of the room. Why had they been left alone? What was happening? The other hostages didn't take their eyes off the screen. Sometimes mild fear is arousing. Sometimes it is hard to know what is arousing and what is not.

'The police found him dead this morning. He died of suffocation, that's all they would say.' Another Mark is dead.

A naked woman is on a metal kitchen chair, she has two cocks in her hands. She puts them in her mouth. Both cocks are hard. The sofa in the background has a big check. I can't make out the colour as it's in night vision. Next, one guy is behind the sofa and is getting his cock sucked while the other guy is slowly easing the head of his dick into her ass. Then all three are on the sofa. She is bouncing hard onto one cock and the other guy is getting his length sucked.

We were told that disturbed sleep, nightmares and insomnia were typical effects of trauma. So talking was good and a way to get the fear out but should be considered an erratic measure of our state of mind. For the next few months we would not be ourselves. We would be hostages.

We were informed that for most detainees a key component of repatriation is dealing with the trauma that comes with being held against one's will.

'We are here to get you back. To take your lives off hold.'

They bundled us into two vans. The red and orange lines down the sides blurring like paint smudged across a fridge.

My mind was numb and I didn't recognise Paddington Green Police Station. I was given a couple of sedatives.

When we first got there we were separated and taken into rooms. It was like a job interview you were supposed to do badly in. Fall apart a bit. Forget basic details. That was what they expected. The officers used pens and hot tea to extract a bit of data. I could have been a collaborator. I had spent a lot of time in Cornwall. Why had I started mumbling like that? Was it code?

TV viewers or those using the net would have known more than me as I was only in one room. I couldn't see through the walls. I heard the conversations between the terrorists and the police but couldn't remember a word of them. All I had worked out was they took more than one room. Spread out to make a storm difficult. Smart for surfers and maybe based on how they hang beyond the breakers in small groups. They probably played a lot of online games. You don't have to go hiking to bond and formulate strategy. There are plenty of virtual spaces to act out goofy plots.

Their plan made little sense but the police debrief helped me take it to another level.

All the cops who dealt with me said similar things. The script was taught to them in a special research unit. They said, 'When you first come out of a captivity situation or an isolation event, you're probably going to have nightmares, sleep disturbances and some fear reactions, but this a normal response to what has happened to you. It's treated as *normal people adjusting to an abnormal event*.'

The Closing Ceremony

'William?'

'Yes'

'It's Lottie.'

'Sorry, I was dozing. What is it?'

'You've been invited to the closing ceremony by the Mayor.'

'I don't want to go.'

'William, don't be petulant. There is nothing to be scared of.'

'I don't want to go. It would look ridiculous. Are the others invited?'

'Of course, Tim arranged it.'

'I forgot about him. Are Kim and Becky going?'

'I don't know. Will you go if they go?'

'I don't know.'

'Do it for me, William.'

'I don't do anything for you.'

'Don't be silly.'

'Are you going?'

'No, but I would see you there. The world will be watching.'

'I don't know.'

'I can't beg William, but I am prepared to bargain.'

'Lottie, I am into someone else.'

'I know that but how about I let you write another novel?'

'What, another real novel?'

'We could do a limited edition.'

'Would I get an advance?'

Bubble Entendre

Swallow

Risible though it sounds, he'd only had one legitimate
occupation. Petrol pump attendant. A summer job in Cornwall
in the summer of 1979. While TV was flooded with the fall
of Mohammed Reza, Shah of Iran, he stood on the forecourt
of a nameless station on the causeway between Hayle and
St Ives. In the summer sun he'd chat to truckers and various
strays picking up fags, sweets, porno mags and petrol. OPEC
was pushing the prices up daily. No one at the station was
complaining. Scams were easy. No one knew how expensive
derv or petrol were. An economy of whims, one might say
to oneself in a moment of Cartesian duplicity.

The derv or diesel was the major earner as the truckers would
'fill up' half-empty tanks and split the difference. It was easy
money. It was theft but not as much fun as servicing ladies
who cruised up and wound down their windows. He was
the new boy, streaks of dark Mobil and Esso Super Lube up
to his elbows and across his naked sixteen-year-old stomach.

She couldn't hear his memories. She was subsumed in
sparkling darkness. Her eyes soldered closed. Two hundred
feet above them kestrels start to screech, circling the tenth
floor of the block and swooping down on bats that navigate
the estate.

He was years away from coming. His hands drifting across flesh, sucking memories from her mouth.

'Check the oil, darling', she'd say and then a hand would stroke his shoulder before a body wedged itself between him, the car and the pumps. Conversations happened as the numbers rolled. Petrol flowed from the source through rubber hoses. Hands miraculously slipped to his cock and retracted in slow motion. Blonde girls, dark girls, good girls, bad girls, dirty binaries slipped back to zero and money was exchanged.

Some girls were addicted to the smell of Four Star. They came back at curious times to spend a few quid on the pumps and buy fags. Never to talk politics. Sometimes he'd let them put the nozzle in and watch as they worked the cranky trigger with their manicured hands. Mostly they pretended he was in control. Their eyes froze in their sockets as he pulled out of their fuel tanks, petrol dripping down the side of the bodywork. In the night air it was an exotic urban aroma. The tidal estuary stank of sewage from the nearby works.

The causeway was the only stretch of fast road for miles and it attracted a community of sorts. Ecologically retarded speed fiends and thrill seekers; Kawasaki riders and rusting Daimler drivers. The entourage was endless and vulgar. Those he didn't fuck were fucking each other. Camouflage school girls and Brut drenched blokes worked curious routines in the back of Capris and other less glamorous Fords. Council housed heroes and their girls next door, driven by Merrydown to go down burping. Shagging was cheaper than cruising.

In the fried fag-butt ambience of the cafe he ate egg sandwiches listening to gossip. A relentlessly meticulous inventory about the form and bits of sluts who were worth shafting. This cruel history inspired the legends written in the shelters, on the streets and the toilet walls. 'Belinda is a slag. She blew off Moose the mouth'. Beirut was a lifetime away and history didn't include Islamic revolutionaries.

The hymns of the city scratch themselves across the concrete in ungainly verse. Pennies and keys inscribe detoured rage and jealousy. You don't need to go Greek to uncover the origins of philosophy. Every neighbourhood has a code to encrypt the laws of desire. The boy's memory was most rudely erased by her fist as she came. He toppled ejaculating and broke her fall.

Still somehow inside her he asked, 'What was that for?'

'You were thinking of someone else weren't you?'

He looked and smiled. A juiced organ flopped out of its burrow. Her eyes blazed on full beam. The rain stopped. The faintest audio efflux crawled around the red walls of the estate. The stereo of a stolen car or the first workers rising. The kestrels had fallen on their prey.

She looked down at her ankle, covered in someone else's shit. A hundred and twenty-two pounds worth of shoe soiled with the spasm of a distant sphincter. The splattered encryption of masticated nutrients. It was sticky rather than tacky like gum. Mastication comes from the Greek for chewing gum. *Mastiche*, pronounced, 'mas ~tee ~ka'. The resin from the bark of the mastic tree. Needless to say most people don't swallow gum.

The azure blues of the Cornish skies receded as they turned on the hall lights and made their way to the kitchen. Godrevy Lighthouse and St Ives Bay already a distant beacon of another kind of story where the summer was nothing but memories strewn over rock pools, where anemones flourish their antennae in ripples of forgetfulness.

It was too late for food and anyway they had left nothing but moulding trash behind them. Silently they drank the only treasure stowed in the recess of the fridge. A couple of bottles of iced blonde beers swilled between drags on a spliff. Stoned they crashed on the bed and slept with the sheets crumpled around their feet, the unburned texts of their funeral robes. Already the repetition was unbearable but they were bound to it.

Tethered sentences hovering over words, levitating rich effluent from the body abandoned to gravity, floating you back on the tide with the lunar precision of a menstrual cycle. Grammatical subversion of subjects sprayed before the waves, erased or displaced across paragraphs and chronological calendars. Improper conjugation. Subliminal locutory slips deposited into sleeping accounts. Oil and cum.

Debts mount up as the economy is calculated. Some returns are more profitable than others. They charge an entrance fee of five pounds to enter Highgate Cemetery. I suppose that keeps the vultures away from the corpses but it doesn't silence the spectres.

Sentences automatically issue from the fissures of the text and place you in front of another ending. A frenzied hand transcribes notes from the other side. The hand is shaking but the words, camera and lights are read with ease. Another iris stopped down to block out the light of the rising sun. Another roll of film exposed to nothing but the noise of a shutter opening and closing. The words look as if they may have always been here. Hidden like lottery numbers behind a thick layer of anticipation. The whirring rhythms of the motor spooling the film, an afterthought, to bracket the narrative within zone systems of philosophy.

Untitled no. 2

Weirdos like to meditate, she prefers to tan. A lot of black girls do, she says. The boy next door was back late last night. There is an ecology of signification which we will digest later. Her breakfast was a cup of Lavazza and what was around. Not much, as usual. After checking her email she left and headed for the parlour.

The estate was quiet. Her Honda Prelude unscathed by a night alone. It started first time, that was why she bought it. Minutes later she was parking, the ash from her first cigarette in her lap. She stepped onto the street and the noise strata opened.

She is a nucleus of propaganda. Her real name is not important. She calls herself Snow White. She wears shades like a droll parenthesis across her face. She walks a cheeky two-step. Her beat a scientific medium that buries itself in cryptic threads to divert you from the beginning of the end, exhaled reluctantly with post-coital attention to the infection of unprotected conjugation. Burial was not her style, too well known, she preferred her dubstep on 12-inch vinyl with white labels.

Her appointment was for eight. She was obviously trying
to avoid the rush in a world where military metaphors are cut
with casual doodles to date an image. The reverse shot tracks
an impacting missive on the field of vision. White noise rushes
through her black head. Its interior copied on hard drives,
a swirl of scars, the organised shrapnel of dissemination, occult
marks shift her figure across the page. Plastic pays for the bed.

One hears the colon at work: it ranks between period and
semi-colon, sometimes used to mark antithesis, illustration
or often with a dash to signify a quotation. She turns, sunlight
filtered by the tinted windows reduces her to a cartoon moving
towards the vivarium: blacker than black. Dreader than dread.

Inside she removes her wrapping. Her figure was soft under
the fur. She picks up her faux reptilian bag and pulls out a
stick of Juicy Fruit and a set of headphones binding a Walkman.
She turns on the tanning tubes and lies on the sunbed. In the
encrypted space of the sentence or epitaph, the chemical
process of transmutation occurs. She chews slowly, the chicle
or latex of the Sapodilla tree releases molecules of flavour.
In the time it takes to smoke a cigarette…Her daydream
empties the latex of its taste. Somewhere Devil's Breath Gum
is mesmerically consumed.

She plays with the gum, turning it over with her tongue.
The random interface toying with the sedimentary city,
the seductive if obtuse inflation of mythology. Mr Wrigley
was a pioneer of product advertisement.

She turns over. Vision tracks around her, shifting between
wide angles and close-ups. A vampire in a blaxploitation film,
she vapourises perspective. The soundtrack is minimal

electronica. Snow White drip feeding herself audio shuffles through bursts of Béla Bartók's *Duke Bluebeard's Castle*.

After some deliberation she selects and reclines. She moves about getting used to the tubes. Fluid and amorphous wavelengths of light dissect the spaces between her flesh and the glass tomb. She reaches for her bag again and extracts a book. An old paperback. She opens it and carries on reading from where she stopped the previous night. She squints in the harsh light and the words click into focus.

'Tuesday March 24th, 1970: "This is one nigger who is positively displeased. I'll never forgive, I'll never forget, and if I'm guilty of anything at all it's of not leaning on them hard enough. War without terms…"'

Her pose might be called electronic demonography. It is not disturbed by the ringing. She merely leans lugubriously over the edge of the luminescent frame and drags a mobile from her bag and lays the book on the floor. The phone glows in her palm.

'Snow White', she purrs her nom de jour.

There is no cutaway to the face on the other end of the line. The other voice is familiar but its intimate tone distorts the identity of the Recording Angel. Nothing disrupts our pleasure in surveying this paradoxical scene, this Black Snow White.

'What can I do for you?', she continues after a long pause filled with the clicking of gum.

'I'm ready to record you', the Recording Angel announces.

'No problem.'

Her words soft and evasive metaphysical epitaphs. Her palate questioning our multicultural agora, evoking the meshworks of belief that have been scrambled in order to create political hegemony.

The voice solicits information. Both voices are female. All identity is erased in this labial annunciation of location. Sex becomes the friction between virtual geographies. All secretions lubricate the background hum that was Snow White's soundtrack. Funk…F static that is.

'Where are you?', the Recording Angel asks.

'I'm tanning myself and reading one of my brother's books.'

'On a beach?'

'No. I'm in London?'

'Oh sorry, I thought it was just a line to evoke something sexy.'

'Yeah right. I'm at home in Hackney with a sunlamp and a big poster of Jamaica on the wall behind my bed…No wait! It's coming to me. I'm on a rooftop in Nefta and you'll need a second mortgage to cover this call!'

'Where is Nefta?'

'It's in Tunisia. It's an oasis.'

'That sounds romantic. What happens there?'

Snow White is in control. She allows silences to envelop her periods. Long silences. Eternal rhetorics of perverse volition.

'Nefta is the spiritual home of Sufism.'

The Recording Angel allows the tape to roll. The information isn't crucial. It is the tone that appeals.

'You mean those spinners. I saw them on a TV documentary. Is that where you wish you were?'

'I don't want be anywhere. I want to become an elsewhere for you. A mirage. I'm the enigma. You decrypt me.' Snow White plays her lines with ambiguous relish.

The Recording Angel watches the needle fluctuate as the words, 'I'm the heir to Malcolm's X', register on the recording heads.

'OK. By any means necessary but let's start with the beginning. Who are your parents?' The other voice now sounds as if it is very familiar with Snow White.

'My mother was a crack whore. She married a dealer whose Porsche she used to fuck a tree. I was delivered posthumously. He remarried an actress who persecuted me so I left home at fourteen.'

'That's so tragic…'

A slightly bored expression creeps across Snow White's rouge lips. She listens to a string of empathetic phonemes but searches for something in her bag. A bottle of perfume. It is difficult to find *Shocking* by Schiaparelli. Her sister brought it back from Cannes before flying out to Columbia.

Demurely, she applies it to herself. Spraying it at targets we cannot see. Just below her belly button, just above her wrists… Her warm flesh shivers and she offers a riposte.

'Oh sweetheart shit happens. She'd smack me up in front of guests, make me perform burlesque tricks when daddy was away. I was fly enough to haul my ass outta there.'

The words are paced with the hiss of point blank impact and the click click rhythms of the gum penetrated by her tongue.

'She was jealous of your relationship with your father?'

'Shit you're sharp. She thought I was competition.'

'Sexually?'

Vision slips into macro on Snow White's fingers as she guides the glass bottle over her blue pubic hair, lightly releasing another puff of scent. The spray causes her to flinch, just slightly.

'No intellectually.'

'Joke right?'

'Some people do.'

'Is that why you call yourself Snow White, because you had a wicked stepmother?'

'Well it wasn't because I fucked dwarfs as a child. Not that I have anything against people of diminished altitude.'

'So how would you read your version of Snow White? Is the Black Forest a metaphor for Snow White's bush?'

Cut to a Nagra tape machine. Spools slowly turning. There is a pause in the dialogue. Dissolve to Snow White.

'My bush is blue actually, but yeah, the story demonises femininity as a strategy to manipulate perception.'

'Are you suffering from *Belle de jour* syndrome?'

'No.'

'Come on!'

'No. You come on. Shoot some more questions. I ain't no bitch blogger.'

'Say something dirty.'

'Fuck you ho!'

Snow White hangs up. She was bored by the caller and returns to the performative process of her artificial tan and pushes up the volume on the opera. Once more she reads from the poorly glued ensemble of pages of her Penguin book.

'Wednesday March 25th, 1970: The more perverse of
"Hitler's Little Helpers" save their excretions to throw in our
cells as they walk back and forth to their shower and exercise.
The shit literally flies at us almost every day. The blacks
don't even consider throwing excrement. We retaliate
by shooting them with little, crudely-made zip-guns and
powerful slingshots fashioned from the elastic on our shorts.'

She has barely processed this paragraph when the phone
rings again. Snow White answers it. Her tone is cool.

'I'd rather talk to the frozen faeces of Freud than have
a one-to-one with you.'

She listens to a voice that is muffled and breaking up.

'What did I say? It seems like the gap between Hackney
and Islington is widening. You're taking this too seriously.
Three months and you really think you're on the menu,
blackberry tart does chocolate sauce. Come on Catherine
it's art, don't be so aggressive.'

'Listen this shit stinks. Talk to my husband. Me, I'm hanging
up, I've some reading to do.' Snow White cuts the caller
off again.

Recording heads. VUs registering the static interface where
electronic voice phenomena are said to cluster. The phone
rings again. Snow White stares at the set of numbers and
then responds.

'If you phone me one more time I'm going to report you to
the police. I've got your number. Find someone else to molest.

I don't care who you think is going to produce BSW. Under artificial light I've said more than enough for you already. Please excuse the dated vernacular. Your attitude is totally whack!' Snow White puts the phone down.

Eclipse

X-rated rays burn a white hole in the blue sky. It was a perfect day for reading black assemblages of letters strewn over the page. We were on the beach.

The sole of the boy's foot fills the frame. Toes buried into the white sand. Obscure cartographic lines traverse the flesh. The sole leads to the ankle and on to the calf. Sounds of the waves corrupted by the faint and distorted melody of *Remember Walking in the Sand*. The leg lay on a sports towel and was joined to the body of a languidly reclining boy. His checked Louis Vuitton swimming trunks clung to him, sand stuck to his cheeks like a pantomime blusher.

Waves broke in the distance.

Beside the boy chromosomes were aligned differently. She stretched as if waking from some laborious dream. Unlike him she was lying on her back. She turned sideways. She had straight hair that looked like a blond broom with brown tints. Her eyebrows were virginal and arched, her eyes were clear and displayed a hint of cruelty. Her full nose and lips conspired to distance him with a pout of arrogance. In the small channel of sand between them she inscribed a Theta sign with a knife.

'What's that? A Mexican on a tightrope?', he asks.

Smiling and slowly sweeping the air with her head, she replies pedantically, 'No. It's Theta.'

She sounded posh but this might have been an affectation designed to evoke sophistication. She could have done elocution to avoid irrumatio but had a lexicon like Sasha Grey and probably loved the occasional skull fuck. She had expensive skin. A beauty spot above her right breast. These were the thoughts that occupied him as he answered her taunt.

'I know.'

'Define it!'

'It's the empty set.'

'The void matrix that brings harmony to chaos.'

'It would make a cool tattoo.'

'Tattoos are too permanent. I don't want a coroner jerking off over my soul scars.'

She leant back and peeled off a smile for him. He turned towards her and picked up the knife. Using the blade as an improvised mode of delivery he layered sand on her stomach. He proceeded to smooth and square off on his leather canvas. Without drawing blood he carved the sign around her heavily lidded belly button.

'What about a temporary one?'

She gazed up into the endless sky. Her body inked onto the sand. A shadow splitting flesh from silicon. The spangly bikini curled over her.

She pushed her fingers into the hot white grains and microscopic shells. In close-up she exhaled a stage school sigh.

'I suppose a temporary Star of David could be five minutes of fun.'

'I saw this bloke with a neat tat.'

The boy turned his head around and pointed to the nape of his neck.

'Crime Incorporated, below a barcode. Really tidy.'

'I'm more into things that fade away.'

'Like erections.'

'Or Life.'

'Life doesn't fade!'

'Doesn't it?'

Her head lolled in the heat. Lips heavier than velvet curtains revealed the stage where enamel showgirls prepared to entertain the gentlemen in the front row. His head glided down on wires. He blew the sand from her stomach. He blew into the depression of her button. She laughed with her whole carcass and her arm reached for the cavity of her bag. She pulled a pack of Orbit from the Prada sack and used her teeth to tear open the package. He kissed her warm belly as she extracted a white stick of gum from its silver foil.

'What else is in the bag, any Viagra concepts?'

'What do you mean?'

'Concepts like good and evil?'

'I prefer the impotency of faint arousal to the chemical dumper truck.'

'Zionist.'

'I said I'd like a Star of David on my cheek didn't I? I've got a biro in my bag. Wittgenstein swore by them.'

'Don't be stupid.'

'I'm not. I think it would look chic.'

Unsurprisingly she failed to blow a bubble with the chewing gum. She wasn't even trying. It was just a reflex. Her face clouded over for a second. The disappointment of another more serious issue. She rummaged around in the bag dragging out a pen and passing it to him.

'Violà! Go on I want to see the eclipse with chaos on my face.'

The boy took the pen and leant closer to her, carefully drawing the sign on her skin. She put her hand on her hip and presented the mark to him. The de rigueur occult symbol.

'How does it look?'

'A bit silly. You look like one of Charlie's Angels.'

'You're just jealous, 'cos you want one.'

'Fuck off, I don't!'

'Have you seen, *Knife in the Water?*'

'What's that?'

'It's a film, stupid. Don't you know anything? It happens on a day like this. Two lecturers pick up a hitcher and take him sailing. It's in Polish but there isn't a lot of dialogue, just a lot of heat. The boy was a bit like you.'

'Why?'

'I don't know. Maybe because you're always preening like a girl.'

The boy tried a mean face. She wasn't impressed.

'You need a Star of David on your forehead. Then you'll look like a nutter.'

'Go on then. Put it between my eyes like the swastika Tim Roth had in *Made In Britain.*'

She tottered over to him and drew the sign on his forehead. He stared at her. Dumbly hypnotised by the pert elevation of her bust despite the flimsy support of the bikini. She scrawled the image between his eyebrows and pushed him down on the sand.

Lying on top of him she asked, 'How long to the eclipse then?'

He looked at his watch. Grey digits read: 10.10am. He looked up at the sky and said, 'Sixty minutes.'

She rolled off him and onto the towel. The boy picked up a 7Up bottle and pointed it at the sun.

The silence bored her, so she infected him with her thoughts: 'The Nazis were into astrology weren't they?'

'I never heard of that!'

'Really?'

'Yeah, really!'

'What are you doing with that bottle?'

'I'm going to use it as lens.'

Something in his expression appealed to her and this time the bag delivered a compact camera. She framed his fingers around the nape of the bottle just below the rim that once retained the top. A silent digit flexing was succeeded by the double action Tchuk, tst. Victorious, she flipped onto her belly and lay waiting for the eclipse.

But she couldn't help chatting and out of nowhere said, 'It was so easy.'

'Like losing your virginity?'

'Sort of.'

She fell silent and an almost serious look passed across her face.

'What?'

'Nothing. I remember the first bloke who had me, had this dog that wouldn't leave us alone. He put on Pink Floyd.'

'No, don't.'

'Honestly. *Dark Side of the Moon.*'

'That's enough to scar you for life.'

'Tell me about it. His fucking dog kept jumping on the bed and sticking its snout in my snatch.'

'Kinky?'

'Maybe it thought it was a bloodhound.'

'You're sick.'

'Just noticed?'

'So how come he didn't tell it to fuck off?'

'I didn't ask.'

A long silence ensued. He thought she looked a bit like Sissy Spacek circa 1974.

No. 2

Quite sublime. Smoke pirouetting on a carpet of sunlight. She had seen sites online dedicated to the predictable fetish of red lips around a stained filter but none really captured smoke. As illusive as an orgasm and flowing according to the most delicate laws of thermodynamics. Exhaling for the sake of the patterns she unwrapped the gum. It looked just like Hubba Bubba but the letters had been altered to *PSYCHO STASIA*. Gone too was the trashcan and in its place was a flaming skull. This was Devil's Breath Gum, made, so the story goes, from the Brugmansia tree.

The purple block looked harmless. She watched the sun dissect another plume of smoke and then stubbed out the last of her Benson and Hedges. The health warning on the packet made her do it. She was dying already for sure. She'd smoked tons of the things. She loved to smoke and chat. It was all she was good at. The gum tasted like nothing special. Late-twentieth-century chemicals. There was no bitter taste or clue to its potency but she was a great believer in hype.

Her mobile was cold in her hands and for some bizarre reason this felt good. She lay back on the white sofa and assumed a pose she had seen below captions such as, THE SOFT, HAIRLESS FLESH OF HER LABIA INTOXICATED ME, AND I SLID MY TONGUE INTO HER SLIPPERY SLIT. The miniature hand-set was soon warm and sticky. Her fingers fluttering over the pubic glow between her legs. Her clitoris stiffened, resembling one of the phone's green buttons. She dialled home: 08980101010I. Her eyes closed, she allowed the object to slip into her cunt and then pulled it out before opening her eyes and sucking it clean. The taste of her own juice was like the sea breeze on Brighton beach. She wanted to talk to someone. For someone else's voice to take her to a climax. She dialled a number. A man answered, 'Luciphone is not at her desk.' She didn't want to talk to voice-mail. She put the phone down between her heels and impaled herself on it. Her circuits were plugged in elsewhere. She was alone on the set, degrading

herself for the police photographers. She knew her corpse
would be poked and dissected for evidence of misadventure.
She was breaking up, becoming the random body dissolved
in venal ecstasy.

She worked the gum about on her fillings and pressed it between
her molars. Her masticating jaw articulated a life story not
unlike your own. Back a hundred days to that morning of the
solar eclipse. Waiting for totality, the appearance of the Corona
and Baily's Beads.

She told herself it was pure curiosity. The stuff that killed pussy.

Pre-coital dissonance squinting through killer Loop shades
at the surfers in the marine-blue swell. They could have been
the ones they'd met at The Shire Horse. The boy with the
rodeo pecks and cute smile who'd sold her the gum. They were
too far out to tell. They were burnt flesh on coloured sticks
of spun glass. Lurking beyond the breakers for a tsunami to
ride in the warm darkness of an August morning. Spitting
salt water theories through sun blocked lips of a lunar current
accumulating in the Atlantic. Dolphins were sending LFOs to
warn of the invisible velocity surging towards them. Anything
to kill the boredom of waiting. Was she ever going to?

They bobbed around. Waiting for that first wave to come like
loitering punctuation marks hanging out for a limousine full
of concatenations, nouns and verbs. If you open those two black
punctures on the front of your face light rushes in. Imagine if
we had conscious control of the iris, could control our exposures
at will. She tensed and released her vaginal muscles around the
object. Her clitoris engorged and fragrant like a Datura head.

The story was dialled out to the last red telephone boxes on the street. She knew that outside they'd be crawling on their hands and knees like Indian mystics, sadhus seeking the truth in the scattered remains of caramelised latex clinging to the tarmac. The story began with a full stop. Full stops don't stop anything. They'd be trying to prise the gum away with their nails. They were wasting their time. Only last week she had been at a do in the country and had fucked a boy beside a pool. Someone had been there before them and left some gum as a keepsake. It had stuck to her Maharishi skirt and then to the seat of the car. It took the same fabric cleaner that almost killed Liberace to get the stuff off. Full stops are like that.

This is the ledger of billions of pounds worth of wasted stock. When all the meaning is chewed out of the book the plot is transmogrified into pure pulp. She knew something at the centre of the void was calling her. It was an invoice of sorts, an inventory of their crimes. A pair of quotation marks giving head. Coming on like clouds as the sun rose towards it zenith.

She wondered how long it would last. Devil's Breath users often failed to realise they were tripping. Only a couple of weeks ago she'd read this online. There was a Schedule D notice on the drug so all the information was being sourced from rumour mills. A million seconds before or more, when the boys in the bunker came, she'd believed those rumours were based on facts. He was open to suggestion. A bit of a zombie.

From: hiedi@altitude.com
Date: Wed 17th June 1999. 7.25pm
To: List@index.org
Subject: This gum thing

This may just be bullshit but I heard NATO has inaugurated
a special squad to; [i]investigate the psychedelic drug
'Psychostasia' Increasingly popular among P.L.Us. A bit
like DMT, the drug became notorious following it's use in the
penal system as a form of voluntary capital punishment and
previously by the CIA as a method for securing confessions.
Now it is supposed to be on the black market. So far the
devotees have come from sectors of the social outside stable
statistical feedback but numbers are rumoured to be growing.
As yet it has not struck at the heart of the leisure industry as
it is not conducive to dancing and results in the death of the user.
six times out of ten, and zombie like states in which anything
ican happen and the user is totally out to lunch. Like wow, it
sounds heavy. Anyone heard anything about it. Is this for real?

Other drugs peak but this was different. She wasn't coming
down. It was a dial tone purring with information. Unzipped
she started to navigate the pixelated labyrinth and laid the
shattered phallus on the scales of Osiris and Isis. A kilo or
two of misdemeanour. Her mouth was dry and her skin ran
with sweat. The spinning room a blurred cocktail of colour.
The voices started…

Her lids fluttered shut, weighted down by her luxurious lashes.
Leaf-green eyes shaded from light. Who was she now? Alone in
the 'evocative fragrance' of Ambre Solaire. Sweet-like chocolate
dripped over vanilla ice cream, her photo-stable chemical cuticle
stroked by his hands. Fingers extended in search of her pollen,

massaged her neck and shoulders. His fingerprints would leave no trace on her.

They paid no attention to the warning on the bottle. They lay in the sun as the shadow encroached. They were the formulaic lines of a porno Bazooka Joe cartoon. Her gelled fist jerked his cock. Up and down her hand slid. Her thumb taking time out to focus on the slit on his joy-stick. Her grip was strong but he seemed miles away. He was back in the boy's mouth. His hands were all over her. She wanted to go back too. Distracted by the silence of the beach she'd forgotten the boy in the void. Now she remembered him. The smell of him on her body as she told him she wanted to fuck him to death. Something in his hair she thought. Something on his skin. Something jealous like revenge.

In the prequel to the eclipse he fingered her. His thumb stroking the manicured stubble between her cunt and anus, merging the front and the back, her clit and her pubes, his 'n' her skin. His mouth and her ear, his words in her cortex, his files on her desktop, his icons in her trash, his cock on her laptop. Soft porn inside her. Outside the dream of her solitude, inside the smooth oiled shaft of her sentence with its spangly bikini straps taut around her thighs, pulling as she pushed herself onto his filthy fingers. Her period brought on by lunar motion and the repetitive pleasure of her pelvis. Her blood dispersed in the Factor 8 oil.

Prisoners were found with their genitals exposed or if still alive beaten to a pulp with no recollection of violence. All genetic models seemed receptive to its equation. Spent gum on the floor beside their open mouths or still clenched between their teeth as if petrified in orgasm. Teenagers alerted the web to the auto-erotic effects. It was all over the chat rooms. It made sense to her. Her clitoris spelt out the code for her fingers to follow.

A black hole at the end of an unreadable sentence snuck between us. Full stop. A period of silence, a cycle of returning marks or traits that structured the fluidity of words which emerged from unfathomable distances, coiling through the waxed cylinders of our recording machines and search engines. The story rewound miraculously as a dot on the sun. An eclipse seen from a sandy beach. Heels pushed the sand back towards the shore while the body allowed gravity to attach an address to unclaimed daydreams. Sand engaged in unknown dynamics of copulation. Granular sentence endings encased in blood and oil.

Her life was ebbing away in the inevitable discourse of the end. The clouds covered the sun. Waves of unclaimed mail accumulated from urls broken by the finite placement of dots. Words randomly plucked from the syntax of the last century were stockpiled around familiar nodes. Dots, not full stops or periods. Although she noticed that '/' also signified the termination of a statement. Thick grey clouds like premature cum soaked the sky. And then through a crack the sun appeared again. It burnt her face as she looked up at the boy. She was squinting and he was pumping her full of ferocious love.

The bottle focused on the page began to smoulder. Time spiralled through geonomic accounts searching for an invoice for the imminent flame. The disconnected line stretched to infinity. Lying on the crumpled sheets of her bed she came again. It was pure repetition. The only certain satisfaction she had ever had in the world. She wasn't touching herself but she felt another orgasm coming. She started to scribble

on a pad. 'I can't stop coming…I've found…I'm sorry it has
to end this way…'

It was a brief suicide note. And probably not what the magazine
had expected when they phoned her and asked her to do an
article on the gum. They should have known better. She should
have begun writing her article a little earlier in the day.

There are no Es in Cult Fiction

Everybody knows the only drawback in dealing is listening
to the constant traffic of drug fiction. On the odd occasion
he has been a rent boy, pornographer and copper. The latter
really shits them up. Sometimes, and that is very rare indeed,
these stories are vaguely amusing.

Take for example the other night. Opposite Chalk Farm tube.
The pub was pants, filled with drones dragging out alcoholic
sentences and postponing a walk home to the tedium of
tomorrow and another day. The walls were plastered with mug
shots of the top stock, Sam Beckett, Jimmy Joyce, ee cummings.
He could go on.

Anyway, he strolled in there looking to down one before
the last bus to NW11. He was feeling pretty sorted after signing
up for a kilo a month with some geezer who gave him a credit
card and url with the first bag of skunk.

It had been a slow ride to dealer Satori's and his profile was
tinged with malevolence. As an agent of smug belligerence
he was scouting for someone to suck into the vacuum
of his implosive perspective. Click the interactive icon.

Boy sitting@bar. Boy was doing some gum in a tan leather jacket and sunflower shades, and reading *On the Road*. Fucking Bong Buddhism he thought, like Gucci, sounds airtight at a distance but would you read it yourself?

'Mmmm, post-*Trainspotting* literature gobbling Gen Xer', he whispered to himself.

He wanted to index some numbers of his own, and so he crept a step closer. A veteran lech he does this shit without spooking peeps. Boy was gagging for it. Sitting there driving through the blotchy text, blown away by the ghost of summer rain on his wind shields. Boy was twenty-two years old, innocent enough to seduce with some off-piste philosophy. So he asked the boy what all the mug shots meant.

'No idea, mate. Sorry.'

'No problem. I just spotted you drifting through *On the Road* and thought I'd ask. Didn't mean to perv on you!'

'No problem. I was given this by my main squeeze. She said I needed to find something spiritual in life. That was before she dumped me for stayin' out too much.'

'Doing what?'

'Clubbing, popping pills, flirting, dancing you know mate— largin' it.'

'She wasn't into it?'

'Used to be but she's got Verved, started whining, the drugs don't work!'

'Yeah, well there is some ugly entertainment out there.
You go west for the eclipse?'

'Yeah, fuckin' tell me about it. I had a VIP pass and couldn't
get backstage. It did my head in all that mystic bollocks.
Cattle prod the E generation!'

'I didn't go 'cos I'd heard the essential festering tip is a re-rolled
roach of a smoke.'

'So do you live round here?'

'No, I'm up from Ealing. I had to see these people who want
to use a tune I've done for a soundtrack.' I lied for the thrill
of blagging a blagger.

'Nice work if you can get it!'

'Yeah, it's for another Alchemical Generation flick with
a fucked-up plot and double doses of cheesy sex.'

'Good money?'

'Yeah, better than royalties from the old white label.
My cult classic.'

'So what was it?'

'The tune was called *There are no Es in a Void*'

'No, sorry mate, never heard of it, what sort of thing is it?'

'Pretty malignant. Out on Warp.'

'Say no more. Meisters of the weird!'

'Yeah there aren't many good Es around at the moment
are there?'

'Yeah, as it happens I've got something with more bhp than
a Mitsubishi if you're interested?'

'I am. How much?'

'To you mate, nothing. You've saved me from the drudgery
of *On the Road*. It's on me.'

Well that is my E story. Boy slipped me the pill and we
necked about three pints and said goodbye. I was so faced
that I forgot to ask the boy his name. I woke up the next
day alone.

(ø)signifies

Luciphone was a wage slave. She was bound by contract.
In the new hourglass economy her assets were always
being exploited.

While doing her MA she'd dreamt of designing a dank and
mysterious underworld full of Priapean satyrs and lubricous
angels. Now she sold flabby websites to what jodi.org called,
'Ugly Corporate Sons of Whores'. She had no choice. She
was hardwired for consumption. Her desires were constantly
upgrading. The alien face that looked out of her VDU was
dreaming of new items to replace tired accoutrements littering
her Fashion Street studio flat.

Her lenses were pissing her off. Today was a cloudy day. There was nothing she could do about it. Some days were just smeary and itchy. She'd been to the bathroom about four times that morning and sat on the toilet with a contact in her mouth. It was while she was in there that her mobile had gone off at her desk. When she got back her number was in the window. Every window displays a horizon. She was surprised. She hadn't phoned for over a week. Luciphone sat down and almost called back but thought better of it. Now she was questioning her decision. It was terrible being in love. You just don't know whose call it is.

'It's your call', Luciphone said to herself.

The phone on her desk rang. She was an absolute believer in her telepathic presence. She could whisper across the Atlantic and get New York agencies to return calls. But she had to be in the right frame of mind. It was a work related call. Some guy wanted her to subscribe to a royalty-free image base. Like fuck she did. When the line cleared she emailed reception.

'Mark, if you can't ditch the trash, don't dump it on me.'

On his first day Mark made a lot of mistakes. He couldn't remember names. They hadn't asked him about his memory at the interview. Memory is a hardware issue but his short-term memory loss was chronic. He put it down to a long afternoon in Penlee Gardens in 1977 chewing the leaves of the datura plant. The girl had phoned for an interview. Mark couldn't remember Sfax's name so he put her through to Luciphone.

Sfax played a tight set, something clicked. The girl asked Luciphone down to Subterrania. Cultural suicide has a certain cachet in our culture and the girl was an adept at transgression.

Her personality was a layered document. Its only constant factor was the blonde hair that reminded Luciphone of a worn brush. Everything else changed daily.

Luciphone put this down to the perks and neurosis of working for the style press. The girl didn't want to be in, she wanted to be way out. She could barely finish her sentences, she was so bored of it all. That said she was happy for Luciphone to finish them for her as she espoused a philosophy of inauthentic subjectivity — if you know what I mean.

Kanal

The Devil's Breath was a hallucinogenic *39 Steps*, a code perfected to erase undesirables. It suffocated the arteries of perception with garbled venal ephemera rushing towards the climax at the EXIL sign. The user was like Hitchcock's vaudeville trickster, opened by a mnemonic voiced from the dark. The gum took over all available neural networks to process the encrypted erotic ciphers. The users' innate onanophilia exasperated and streamed into a final exquisite replay of the Orgasm Death Gimmick. The speculation following leaked autopsies was that the brain melted to a primal pulp, a gunk not unlike the cachet of this pharmakon.

Technology colludes with distance to deliver disconnectivity. According to the net the death toll was hundreds and rising. The news on TV and at the centre of the web was still silent. It was as simple as that. The net is the perfect agora for phantoms to circulate. Heads without bodies mutating philosophies according to their specific niche, networking through the and/or gates of reality and virtuality to create the immanent interface. The fictional actuality of the dot lexicon blown to infinity like the nets of Yayoi Kusama.

The softwar was over. He was dropped off on Roman Road near to the tube. The Bethnal Green tube sign was splattered with pollution. Somehow the boy knew that his girl was a silent statistic. Why else was she offline? She had done the gum. He didn't suppose that she knew any better than him. Perhaps she thought she could handle it. It was not really fatal, just heady hardcore. Where had she scored? He didn't have the answers. He didn't give a fuck.

At Liverpool Street he changed tubes. His mobile was going off. He was whispering into the handset. No one could hear him but that made him look suspicious. He knew you were supposed to shout. His clients would meet him at Temple. Everyone needed to get out of town for a while. At least until the heat was off. The handset went dead.

Waiting at the turnstile while someone kept feeding a ticket into the machine he wondered if he would ever see his shadow again. His travel card functioned perfectly and he headed for the Circle Line. Into the tellurian flow. He couldn't help thinking about the boy in the void of the bunker. How his girl had watched the dying boy sucking his cock. At least they were there for him. He had someone to experience the end with. He hadn't seen the dying boy pass gum to his girl but he hadn't been paying much attention. He'd been too busy fucking his face, pulling his malleable head to and fro.

They say the gum is a *Rollerball* emission. The boy was hungry for a protein fix and he'd shot deep throat. The dead boy was just another blank page now. Another outline

to be slowly filled at some future date. A string of digits
in an abstract storyline, a triumph of the imagination.

Did the boy pass a wrap? He didn't know but he couldn't get
the question out of his mind. Travelling down the platform
he reflected on the drug's potent empathetic affect. The adverts
tried to short him, Fuzzz, Fuzzz, Fuzzzz but he was fused.
He remembered the body suddenly collapse on the crisp
packets and coke cans, spunk dribbling from the lips.
The eclipse was an anticlimax after that. In the silent chill
of that darkening hour he'd felt a bit spooked like everyone;
but his girl had seen him jack off in the face of a zombie,
and that distracted him from the spectacle.

The tube was chocka. He looked at the floor covered in
gum. It was probably varieties of Wrigley's and a bit of the
competition. Curiouser and curiouser it seemed, embedded
on its flat grey page. You never see anyone spitting the stuff
out. They must do it. Which goes to show how sly humans
are. What tiny per cent follow the instructions for disposal?
Who is the world authority on gum, deadly or otherwise?
It seemed to be one of the quintessential habits of the twentieth
century. A rebellious and moronic pleasure. In the right
mouth it advertised a vacant libido. It was an oral gymnasium
for French techniques. Its functional sugars and sweetness
insufficient to justify its status. Now it was lethal. She was
dead. How could he think such thoughts?

The packed carriage halted at Mansion House. Again more
people got on than off. You could taste the paranoia in the
confined space. He looked at this mass of flesh waiting
to be crushed and wondered how many of them were
in the trade. The paradox being that you can't spot dealers
in a crowd. They are the crowd. The pinstripes and beige

suits didn't fool him. Traders always employ Blendovista™
software to create that flawless encrypted personality.
On a more philosophical tip he knew we are all dealers.
All of us hustling numbers. At Temple he pressed the red
bordered box. The doors opened and he stumbled onto
the platform.

Arriving at the station distracted him from the other passengers.
He heard a soft clap and it startled him. He looked down
on the platform. A light tome had landed on the word GAP.
The demarcation line arched around on the side of the spine.
The rough concrete emphasising the contemporary symbiosis
between the jacket design and the milieu of its reader.

Outward appearance. Lauren Bacall dressed down in frayed
and baggy denims with a natural straw Buddha crop. Bones
modelled in balsa wood but finished in a smooth topping
of caramel flesh. Cool grey eyes stare into infinity, perhaps
she is short-sighted. Maybe she reads too much.

Inside information. She is a waitress at a vegetarian restaurant
to pay for her final year at Brighton University. She is studying
illustration. She stole the book from a bloke she met at the
restaurant. She pretends not to notice when men stare at her.
It doesn't help.

What is she doing or thinking? She does a bit of part-time
modelling to make contacts and she is on her way to a shoot
at the N3 demonstration. She is wondering if this geezer
is going to say sorry for knocking the book onto the platform,
pick it up or just stand there gawking at her.

He downloads a fractured smile and picks up the paperback. The book is entitled *253*, and as he returns it to the girl, the boy wondered if this might be a cryptic reference to the Marquis de Sade. Their eyes almost strayed into communicative exegesis.

Cathode Wounds

Televisual diversion. Inside the Stock Exchange the floor was littered with apocalyptic reams. The flash yellow coat of the dealer jarred with the backdrop of St Paul's. He rocked backwards and forwards repeating kabbalistic jokes to himself, and offering cruel ripostes to cunning punters.

'Fifteen quid to the boys and a tenner to the girls if they blow me off. No honestly, it's the best bubblegum in the world. You transform its value through respiratory dialectics then you die all trippy and spiritualised. I'd give it away if it wasn't such an earner.'

A big black Merc pulled up and its window opened pumping out a pirate station. A charred hand emerged and exchanged cash for the Hubba Bubba clones. They could have been anything as the media never tires of whining. It was *PSYCHO STASIA*. Who would queer a pitch by dealing shit?

Of course you recognise Orpheus shaving in front of the wall of mirrors. He imagined he looked like Al Pacino in *Scarface.* Such is the perverse vanity of the ponce. You think his jacket looks like the one Cocteau wore in *Le Testament d'Orphée.* You realise that everything is seeping through the screen. Another millennial birth.

Shola has followed Kula with the trolley into the lift. Sirens sounding in the distance. The riot squad ferried into the affray, special effects and big beats rocking the block. Have you read *Richard III?* The lift doors close. Fingers elongated closer to the lens guide a masked figure into the room. A Queen for Mayan spirits hovering over the iced head of Trotsky. She pulls open her dress and has syringes for nipples. She arches her back and stops in front of a mirrored wall.

The razor traced contours of Orpheus's reflection. A white room minimally furnished. The geomantic key pauses the frame. The cursor moves to the left and clicks onto a Victorian glass-mounted slide of a dead insect. Below the body the text is blurred out of focus.

The frozen passengers look like they are resisting play. As if they were merely extras in Version 1.0. Were they all agents of SERIAL? The tellurian economy is dead. It would be prescription only in the future. Orpheus looked at her in the mirror. He had seen her lunge through the door wearing high black heels, blue pinafore dress, skull mask and straw blonde wig.

Stokrotka: I hope I don't stink!

Orpheus: If you didn't loiter in the sewers you'd smell
               sweeter but it's your life. I thought you were
               coming back last night?

Stokrotka: I missed the last tube.

The mask is torn off and thrown to the floor. Stokrotka is her code name. She is an agent for SERIAL. She is modelled

on a character called Daisy, in the film *Kanal.* The Agent must
have a name in which the other can believe. Her name sounded
exotic but was meant to sound English. She mocked his tetchy
tone. His voice broken up into indistinguishable resonances
by a pirated audio plug in.

Orpheus: Where did you get that?

Stokrotka: Somewhere.

Orpheus: Which orifice paid for that?

Stokrotka: You tosser. I only came back for you.

Orpheus: For me. Why?

The Mercedes parked in front of the Brixton Academy. On
the streets various social problems hustle fags and cash. Inside
Zebra, and his lieutenant are nervously waiting for some support.
A bird in the back fondles her laptop. Bullets. Sex. Flesh.
Noise. Dead dada's dead. Anita Pallenberg strokes her pussy
and her finger slips into the opened skull of Donald Cammell.

Barefoot the real Daisy strides towards the Merc. The window
slips down. She wears a Mini Mouse t-shirt and is chatty
with Zebra. Her gestures are replayed in the bodywork of the
car. She spoke, intoning details of previous deals in Morocco.
Kilos and then tons of black imported on yachts. She doesn't
stick on details, she's no fucking spy. She just conveys the
mood of it. She draws some figures from the shadow. Smokey
and Trippy, they could have been Dopey and Sneezy but that
was not the point.

Trippy:	Have you got a phone in there?
Zebra:	Why don't you use one on the street?
Trippy:	Come on don't be tight man. Give us your phone for a minute. I need to call Fashion Street.
Zebra:	Are you fuckin' stupid. Fashion Street went before Old Street, you're wasting your time.
Lieutenant:	Just get in the car.
Zebra:	Adrianne move up and let the boys in.
Adrianne:	So did you sort me out a tool Smokey?
Smokey:	Yeah, it ain't much but it'll take someone out.

Smokey has no problem in locating the small gun and passes it over to Adrianne. She looks a bit pissed at its toy-like appearance.

Adrianne:	Is it real?
Smokey:	No it's a heavy water pistol!

Water Margins

Gosh, Gosh, Gosh! There it goes again. A word lifted with a scalpel and laid on the knee of the blind girl, You-shi for the famous model Ke-qing. They have dropped their wannabe weird friends and are alone with deathgum-bubbleyum.

Like Sharon Stone on fourteen figures she raised her St Sebastian arms, replaying the sacrificial pose for the boy in the Golden Temple. Blood, drugs, porcelain flesh stripped bare to the bone. Razor buzzing on dual alkaline batteries. Orpheus toppled into the ritual. There was no play at concealment. The medium of porn is digital video and the Canon XL-1 was premier kit. She squeezed and pouted her grotesques to the beat. She programmed her movements and spasms. She let her body be endlessly logged and compressed in after effects.

Renewable sources of gum. That was the ecological strategy of Wrigley's. Back in 1933 they pioneered WASTE awareness. Please dispose of your gum and the wrapper with care.

Zebra: Here Trippy I got this for you. You're probably stoned enough to play it now, how about a tune?

Trippy: What the fuck is it?

Zebra: It's an ocarina. South American I think?

Trippy takes the instrument and tries to work out where his fingers ought to go. He isn't very successful and only gets rudimentary blowing noises out of it. He hands it back to Zebra.

Trippy: Mind blowing reverb.

Smokey: You really are a bit fucked up!

Trippy: [*starts reciting resonantly*] 'See a land of heavy dreams and shadows…'

Zebra:	Stop playing the fool.
Adrianne:	Cool down guys we're drawing attention to ourselves.

She knew that You-shi had fallen asleep, exhausted by the efforts of their composition. She put the book down and took out a donor card from her pocket.

'Do you want to help others experiment sexually after your death?'

She read the questions and as she had done earlier she laughed silently to herself.

Turning off the light Ke-qing left You-shi and phoned her wannabe weird friend, Bao-yu. She told him about the member of the Neoist Alliance who had given her and You-shi Necrocards earlier that night on the Portobello Road. She told Bao-yu how nervous he had been when he realised that You-shi was blind. Bao-yu laughed at the story. They always had more fun than he did.

The Cocktail Party

Coshed by fear he woke up from a nightmare. He was nowhere already. No photos exist of the garden party. Cocktails were being served in a glasshouse by flamingos. The trays were empty but the birds had an obscure look in their eye. No. He was at Kew, it was after one of those parties she'd invited him to.

He had found a bag of pills abandoned by the invisible hand. He'd given them away at a house party and done some himself.

In one room there was a washing machine tumbling clothes. It phased strangely with the music of Aphex Twin. Before long the pills were being dropped remorselessly.

Sucking a huge technicolor cock. The skull opening its white petals. He couldn't get the sticky psychotropic gobstopper out of his mouth. He was playing with it, pulling it between his lips and then disgorging himself. Never successfully as this was the stickiest testicle of gum. It just fell around in his mouth. Intense colours twisting and congealing, evolving into ever-more ludicrous forms in the foam. Infinitude gum, psychoanalytic gum, philosophical gum. The kind of stuff that sticks in your interpretive membrane. It was caught in his mouth, an obscene joke he couldn't laugh at.

Adhering to this dream rebus the gum vanished behind a silk handkerchief. Inside a Victorian conservatory he looked up and saw giant phallic fungi—chroma blue stinkers. The spores fell on the summer breeze that had crept into his sleep, covered his face and shoulders in their sticky, pungent seed. He was snoozing on the Circle Line. He woke up. Nobody had noticed. The passengers were strung out on an infinity of operations. Undercover agents for the corporation. Mr Wrigley and the others. Mr Drug. They were all there but they weren't after him. His laundry was not the problem. It was the economy. A phantasmagoria fading to a white dot. Post transmission the incredulous content of the dream seemed portentous.

Orpheus and Stokrotka. They were players in some nouvelle vague version of events. Subtitles, acoustic traces draw the user down into the colon: into the void of the city and the dead screens. It is a game. You read the text back and filter the information. Insert the missing scenes by cross-referencing the novel and the CD-ROM.

Not that you have to play such retro games or re-read the history of media art in the 1990s. There is no tomb in York for the idiom or chiasmus from which to start the story. There is no point. The police are grabbing people at random; although obviously not the smartly dressed drones.

The screaming on the underground echoed. The tube doors squeaked like rats with seats for jaws. He was deep in the jungle surrounded by the Zapatistas. Screeching modems surrounded him; rebels cursed their Dreamcasts after another day on the battlefield of TOYWAR. The beating wings of madness were flapping in the empty stalls, voices were opening up all around him. The unedited babble of angels. Wounded rhetorics of protesters and security.

AVARICE.COM wanted him to subscribe. The nu economy was vicious and virtual. He was part of it. They should be able to smell it. Or sense it. But he couldn't trust their intuition. In the violence, in the rush of pain, in the affray of uniforms and flesh—he felt like part of the mob. He was thrown against the wall and cracked. He wanted to say, 'I'm with you. I want to accumulate wealth.' But he didn't get a chance. He was punished for saying nothing. You have to stand somewhere. Just being is not enough. Desire is already flowing beyond you, subverting the reality of the dream.

Stokrotka: This is our station.

Orpheus: You know one thing you missed growing up
                in Poland?

Stokrotka:	No, tell me?
Orpheus:	*Survivors.*
Stokrotka:	A TV series?
Orpheus:	Yes, it was.
Stokrotka:	Try and walk Orpheus. Tell me about TV later?
Orpheus:	I can walk.

The underground was a popular destination for nomadic dealers and their acolytes. A few bubbleheads could be seen wanking on the tiled floors. The mob derided them. The mob is not so ethereal as to commit suicide for the buzz, it demands the numb reality of free future… unless you're free, the machine will be prevented from working at all.

He wanted to get out of London. The sooner the better. You can't rush a riot. Once it starts it has its own momentum. As above so below. The police struggled with a pandemonium they had sparked.

Orpheus and Stokrotka arrived at Temple as the last remains of the financial cohorts fled. There they were met by Zebra, Adrianne and Smokey, but no Trippy.

'No broken hearts or syringes full of clichés?', Zebra yelled as Orpheus was dragged down the platform by Stokrotka.

Still in the blonde wig and now chewing gum. The track officials were watching their monitors, uncertain when to strike. Dialogue ran to the end of the first take.

Stokrotka: Come on let's get out of here.

Orpheus: It's different for everyone.

Stokrotka: What is?

Adrianne: Love?

Smokey: Madness?

Zebra: The drug?

Orpheus: Death.

Stokrotka: Shut up.

Orpheus sat on the platform. They all looked at him. Stokrotka knelt beside him.

Orpheus: A horse, a horse, my kingdom for some horse.

Endings…

He knew his future was in temporal exile. In the abyss where thought has no substance. In spaces where gum is tediously worked into exhausted sculptural baroques before being secreted for another user. This gum fad won't last. Eat me. Chew me. Blow me. Spit me out or swallow. He could buy a period return. She was dead, he knew it. He didn't believe in reincarnation. She wasn't answering his emails. She had done the gum and rubbed herself out.

At Waterloo the police were being heavy-handed but he had stopped sweating. He loitered around the magazines letting himself become like the others, immersed in the things and flesh that coveted their page space. Escapism was easy. At first he felt like one of those sad POWs at the end of *The Great Escape*. Donald Pleasance in his crappy specs thinking he was almost free when in fact the horizon was a swarm of darkness about to envelope him. It was just paranoia. The negative pull towards a pessimistic outlook. He bought a ticket and headed for the train.

He walked confidently past the police and ticket inspectors using a crafty cockney gait to disturb their concentration. On the Eurostar the mood was edgy, maybe they feared a People's Global Alliance attack. It was like Dianagate all over again. The drones thinking out loud. It was a terrifying silence, a scatological evacuation of the city. The crossing itself was an Op Art journey — Version 0.0 — London and Paris fused like Brighton and Hove. An assault on *A Tale of Two Cities*. An enema emptying the body of its prejudices against speed.

At Saint Lazare he checked out his destination. He was in exile but his desires were not re-routed. A girl walked across in front of him. Blonde hair stroking her waist, a bubblegum pink mini barely covering her booty. It rose magically to display her cheeks. Lecherous phantoms groped her nubile architecture. Her hand listlessly pulled the skirt down, used to these spectral solicitations.

Replicant hero of *À Rebours*, he should have opened his eyes and found himself asleep in a London bar. Unable to make the train journey beneath the Channel you should have let him wake stiff and incur insults and brutal arrest. It would have been too cool. He could have ordered iced tea and slept in the soiled seat of the old cinema. He might have been spiked with a stick of Dentine or some other oral trick. Suppose he found himself chewing wheatgrass in Notting Hill? He looks like everyone else at the turn of century. Obsolete. His laptop battery only powers the machine for two hours before it needs recharging. The Express is pretty smooth. It should have happened years ago. Totality. The Gum.

The hotel room was small. Floral motifs wilted on bedspreads strewn with dead clothes. A mother sodden with tears. She wanted to get out that night below the sign of the plough. She had to wait another day. Her husband had business to do. She was sowing the dreamer's bed with roses. He was beating her back with thorns. Blooded shots rewound of amputated stalks, the smiling murderous youth talks of his war. The reporter on the other channel said, 'Death is a tangent launched remotely.'

Then her daughter entered dragging a friend. Teenage girls in a promiscuous abuse of clothing. Black apparel floating over cream flesh. The daughter looked at him. Nabokov nestled in the cleft of her tongue. Stopping in front of her mother she asked if he wanted to come with them. She would turn the pages for him and read the words with cute derision.

She aroused his sympathy. He agreed to see what he could find out. He left the hotel and the stillness of dawn was ripped apart by gunfire. He started running. Soldiers were corralling people, telling them to take this road not that. He ran through a shop of some kind and found his way back to his people. They were discussing the possibility of staging a film. They asked if he would be interested in directing. He said he wasn't sure. Didn't

they know what was going on? If he wasn't interested they
would shoot without him.

Meanwhile the mother and her family had arrived. He left
with them. She was crying. They took him back to the holiday
village to pick up their things. It was a refugee camp. Singing
was cut up by rounds of machine gun fire. Why hadn't they
brought their things? He looked around in trepidation, panic
rising like a water table. He was as shot as them. They left
the village and headed back across the city. By this time the
city was tripping. All the frames of news recovered from
the corpses of dead journalists had been racked up on DVDs
and were playing back simultaneously.

Everywhere humans engaged in a primal scene of violence,
pulling a trigger or running from a blade. A body is raped
with its own severed limb. The wailing is intolerable. Tears
spun into melody, a stick to hold off madness.

At an embassy building they were pushed into a lift.
Unfortunately the girl and her friend were separated from
the dreamer, mother and husband. Then just as the doors
were about to close and the lift descended...

We'll never know, he was summoned out by a man in a military
uniform. The dreamer had no proper papers. He couldn't
leave in the lift. He'd have to make his own way out. On the
streets adrenaline simulated the effects of an_____
über-amphetamine. He ran behind a local crowd into the alleys
of the city. Opening doors to houses in search of routes away
from a pursuing mob. He remembers entering a house behind
a boy who called into the chaos.

'Are you friend or foe?'

He sprinted through an arcade in which heavy machine guns were expertly emptied by killer kids at distant targets. Through gaps in buildings he saw heavy armoured vehicles firing. Miraculously none of this crossfire hit him. He found himself in a space not unlike the Westway. In a slow-moving carnival crowd. Out of this crowd a woman said, 'I saw you at_____ doing a reading. You were all right. You got a light geezer?'

He thanked her and asked what she was doing in Portobello Road. She said, 'we', picking out faces with her finger, 'flew over to celebrate that bloke's birthday.' The crowd broke into a trot, then a stampede. It was closing in. They had to get to the underground. He split from the girl and her crew and charged down a cream-tiled passageway. He swerved past a man obstructing an exit saying, 'No you can't go down there it's too easy to seal off.'

He ran down what seemed like a crushed escalator. At the bottom a small group was turning around enveloped in smoke. He sprinted back up the stairs and careered off through the maze of tiles and adverts. He joined a group peeling open a locked door and found himself in a vault. At the far end he could hear others trying to enter. He dashed through the space to discover who was attempting to break in through the other door. The metal gave way and two huge fellas fell through the hole propelled by drunken bodies. One of them had shades on. Both slumped against the wall with hideous grins. They'd been bathing in psychotropic gas fermented at Dachau. The dreamer pulled off the shades and peered at a Siamese eclipse layered across a face. He held his breath as if inhaling something combustible.

This precipitated a lurch and a laugh followed by an acrobatic tour around chamber walls. Laughter spread through the posse. One of them started shouting a raucous song, 'Going underground, Going underground…' Another pulled himself up on the railing opposite the dreamer and said, 'Wake up star, it's the end of the line.'

Zombies

Another night of zombies flying through antiseptic corridors. The speeding and jangling trolleys, skidding on the corners. Vertical pilots gagging for air at fixed altitude, unmasked fluorescent tubes casting their urine wash. It was thousands of miles from the soft chaos of the Islington wards I used to work on. Kennedy Hospital, Bogotá was a laboratory analysing the molecular interface between the CIA and the factions who've succumbed to its traps.

Some of these niches are notorious, such as cocaine. But over the last two months the emergency wards have begun to resemble graveyards, zombie shops full of cadavers deposited by cops tired of executing the resistance on behalf of the government. Not that these zombies are dispossessed, on the contrary, they seem rammed to capacity with fractured instructions and narratives. They are screaming wrecks so naturally their stories are no secret. Their fictions were ignored at first. Then slowly I'd find myself stripping a bed with another nurse and she or he would start to make connections.

'Did you hear about the senator and his wife? They had walked for two days, zig-zagging the city pulling cash and handing it over to some street gang.'

'Yeah, I heard that', I'd say in the casual tone that nurses perfect, saturated as we are with the meat of hysteria on a daily basis.

From my childhood I remembered Catherine and I watching old Hammer films. The pretty girl with her cleavage and gown would travel to some remote region with her groom. There either Dracula or some other agent of demonic persuasion with a hypnotic gaze would steal the beauty from her lover's grasp. Catherine used to get scared and cling to me. My sister was terrified of vampires and zombies. I, on the other hand, used to read horror novels such as Bram Stoker's *The Lair of the White Worm.*

As the cases of burundanga intoxication proliferated I was almost tempted to phone London and get Catherine to fly out. She was attempting to write about her teenage life as a white girl in a black skin. When I talked to her neither of us were really sure how we felt about race. When we were young we tried to ignore it. But as we grew up we grew apart. She bleached her cultural roots and I darkened mine. It was probably something on TV that changed her. That would be typical. I'm not being cruel but she loved TV. When she was little our mum would have to drag her back from the screen. She used to like the static tingling on the end of her nose.

Anyway I think her writing is probably a mourning for the end of UHF transmissions rather than a confrontation of her genealogy. I wanted her to see these real zombies wandering around my wards. You'd sit them down and they would be buzzing on this stuff and spieling nonsense that was probably the truth about how some girl had given them some bubblegum or a drink of Coca-Cola and they didn't know where they'd been or why they were covered in blood. They'd just keep circling slowly back to the fact or fiction that a stranger had met them at a bar and spiked them. Several claimed the man who'd done this had introduced himself as Steve Peregrine Took aka The Phantom Spiker.

Saliva smears on a couple of prostitutes found at the scene
of an assassination showed traces of alkaloids, atropine and
scopolamine. Atropine is found in deadly nightshade, just
one of the many plants that like datura are found not just
in South America but back home in England, if not naturally,
then in parks and gardens like Kew.

Plants like these were the fuel that deranged the witches
who were a pagan inspiration to the psychedelically inclined
masters of Hammer. Catherine and I loved to play out scenes
when mum went to work as a nurse. We were both great as
a Voodoo Priestess. The plant sprayer created that sheen of
perspiration, while the flash of the Polaroid would simulate
atmospheric lightning. I suppose I came to Columbia to forget
those games, to finally face the truth of the world. But the
truth is never easy to face. It is always offering you profiles
in different lighting and mise en scène. Here I was in the
midst of a crime wave executed by puppets who appeared
to be character actors in a remake of *Plague of the Zombies*.

Set Theory

Paper is dead. Books are descendants of magic shrouds which
once wrapped the Pharaohs. Post-Y2K. Laundry boy has
returned from exile although he doesn't feel at home in himself.
He sold his dot com and artworks on eBay and had been writing
a novel. This was contrived through a series of interactive
correspondences online under various aliases; fuckface@
hotmail, looseteen@gmail, lonelygirl@ btinternet.com, lost-
boy@googlemail, solaranus@Athye.net, and with others whom
he found through the random pursuit of anyone answering
to; fuckface@hotmail, or janet@ deathgumbubblegum.com,
or john@deathgumbibblegum.co.uk.

The denouement of this journey began:
www.deathgumbubbleyum.com There you can subscribe
to the final revelations and other exclusive offers. A series
of remixes by *Les plumes de jour*…hypertext cartographies
of a non-linear fashion.

South Sea Bubble

The City lights kissed her face. She was lost in thoughts of
elsewhere. She brushed away the noise of conversations with
a swish of her hair. She had spent three months in post-mastic
trauma. She felt fragile but alive. It was not a suicide drug.
It just shook you up a bit and left you open to suggestion.
We are all open to suggestion. We are always straying off the
path, but as Mike Tyson said, 'That which doesn't destroy me
makes me stronger.'

She was waiting with her coffee in an embossed polystyrene
cup. She swept her head around in an arc to check out the
others. They were there to listen to a reading. A celebrity
author whose prescient notes on the everyday were in no way
parallel to her infamously cocotte oeuvre, 'You are the cipher
for a death becoming. I am not a man I am the bomb.' Her
memories of the author had faded and she was disappointed
to discover he was merely an upgrade of the dealer she'd fucked
all those months ago. This particular celebrity was so in love
with himself he could barely read his own (ghost-written)
text. He flirted with the audience, dropping dope references
and cuntish modalities of speech. He told anecdotes about
his escape at the end of the century, and attempted to hide
any sign of commitment to the product piles displayed on
the bookshop floor.

Celebrity author number 9847590 was flanked by publicity agents and the nocturnal emission of foul aphorisms he'd used to seduce her were entirely absent from his patter. The only fact that mattered to her was she'd been totally deleted from his life story. She didn't even figure as a marginal vector. My ex did gum. She wasn't surprised. It was oddly reassuring. A negative affirmation, to be prosaic. A new status. Blank. She joined in the applause, adding insincerity to anonymity. The others thronged around him offering frigid copies up for his defilement. She made an exit failing to notice his forlorn gaze muted by the glass and the loving eyes of a lanky kid.

She didn't miss the paradox of their distance. She had not been with him as she promised on New Year's Eve. Instead she had spent it with the other patients on Brighton beach. After a month she was able to remember bits of her life. She shared these fragments with the others since they helped disprove the rumours. Collectively they decided that the truth was out there somewhere. In the cold euphoria of that December night she had let go of paranoia. She watched the drunken and drugged embrace, engulfing the pebbles of paradise. With the nurses as protection she had mixed with the masses, tasted their Krug and vodka, danced to new beats and seen lovers fall naked into the waves.

At midnight she had been part of that mass murmur—That is it? Now we're bubbled? Yes. The end? An explosion of fireworks over the Palace Pier and rockets which carved crude digits: TWO, ZERO, ZERO, ZERO into a night blue sky.

Come–Mister Trippy Come Again Mix

Mnemonic Fetishes

I began to write a story about the seductive depth of the smile. The smile particular to a digitised image. This is the story that lost the plot. What remains is the fiendish glimmer of an emerging story: a stroke of genius and the strophe of representation. 'No Mona, no more!' Mick Farren's voice screams down the telephone.

Where was i? In the lower case already, spiralling down into the infinity of the origin, the fort da, the joy of departing returns, the dejà vu of narration in this misc en scène of seduction.
I drift with galleons laden with treasure across familiar tropics. The ocean is space. Undulating waves of differentials.

The phone rings. 'Hello? Yes. Yes. No. Don't ask.'

The book exists only as a nexus for nostalgic cartographies.

'And it's always been about an inflatable doll?'

'Yes.'

'I told you the story last year?'

'Yeah, so what?'

It is a simple story. It's set between Brighton, London and Paris. It is an English text with French subtitles. It's a love story. The inflatable body of Dolly Savage: the cosmological memoirs of a prophylactic interface between subjectivity and seriality, surrealism and sensationalism, a ribbed invagination and artificial insemination. She had a genius for melodrama and a penchant for Stentorphone, pretty ethnics, guns, Gucci, garage, bondage, psychoactive nutrients, deviant mail-order mags, manga video, and perpetual access to excess.

I babble into the receiver about the exchange between film and painting, invoking animated drawings by Natalia. 'Simulation is upon us when we believe in pure transcendent categories: God, genius, man, the dream has us in its bind.' I hang up tired by this repetition, by the trivia that has besieged my story. I knew that my flight of rhetoric had been decrypted by their spies.

As the page becomes warmer I forget about the telephone messages, the stories that are enveloping the trajectory of DS. A body drifting fascinated by the distortion of the mirror. The perfect calligraphic inversion that binds the reflections of the Renaissance to this spaced o-u-t zone system and its rigid architecture between the original and the copy.

Leonardo filled his notebooks with observations of perverse and universal insight. Accounts and failed projects: the mysterious line of the creative genesis, the fragmentation of the pedagogy in the ascent of the individual, from bit part in Vasari to centre stage in the genealogy of the war machine.

Come is the title of the book that Dolly is reading. Mark called her DS for short. DS is a stranger sometimes. She reads while others talk. She is listening to what they say and mixing their narratives with her own. She slips into the words on the page and draws you into the lubricated text. She stands on the tube from Victoria to Charing Cross. The date is October 1988. Culture is a flashback to the evolution of discourse.

DS is on MDMA. Heaven is a nightclub surrounded by whores and dropouts. History is a memory cell overloaded with fashion tips. DS, she's not slack. She comes out when you are depressed. She loves dance music and the underground vibe. She is an anonymous part of the crowd. She waves her hands in the air and belongs to infinity. When the price is right she'll score Es for her mates. Dealing in clubs makes her feel nervous.

In the 1990s, history, like many disciplines that evolved in the nineteenth century, had only a vague, popular meaning. In the secret files of the universities other schematic paradigms were being written. DS is a member of a cult that a historian might believe encapsulated the era. The pleasure-seeking miscreant totally clued-up on the capital tip. Spinning around the club scene like a ball on a roulette wheel, she unloads her stock and networks a niche.

Everyone likes to gamble and as MC Kinky said, 'Everything starts with an E.' MDMA is a psychotropic drug. It makes you smile. DS loves the way she feels as the code pulses through her. She loves the energy of the other dancers. On this particular October night, DS is rushing off her tits and standing in line with the others.

Nightclubs are the airport terminus of the pleasure principle. Travellers are body searched as they have little luggage. One is rarely strip-searched in clubs. The truth is never chic. Dreams of flight are thought to be sexual. The dream declares a desire to transgress, to break with gravity, to scribble wings and become animal. Freud saw in Leonardo's helicopter drawings a new model for biographical writing.

Bouncers reassure the punters with a whisper, 'It's alright, we're looking for weapons.' A molotov of memories and laughter. She moves through Heaven with petrochemical allure. Several exposures are rendered obsolete by the virtual confessions of cyberpunks but you remember the look. The sensation of the real thing, body and soul on a trajectory of impulsive nihilism.

The DJ is psychoactive, rewording the connections that have relapsed. The body responds to his biogenetic precision, as if possessed by a Loa of the Voodoo cult.

Magical electricity conspires in Heaven, lights and projections detail the surface. Jeff Koons says that God is in the details. Artists like quoting artists. The image is a stroboscopic effect of a body without organs. A transgressive fiction of escape routes and a pharmacopia for cool mediums of knowledge.

I imagine the story orbiting me. He wrote this story about a sex toy. One of those gross mail-order items. He's a real sick fuck. You know that the Japanese are into those inflatable dolls. I saw them in a magazine called *Flash*. Salarymen will part with a lot of yen for a smooth-seamed model!

'People don't talk about "smooth-seamed models", they talk about TV!'

'So what?'

'So who's going to talk about DS?'

Everyone talks about DS. She is on the dance floor. Everyone is dancing and sweating. Functional semiotics of bodies in rapture. DS is in a flashback. A virginal time of slow striptease. The event is formatted and the digits logged. Brighton beach at sunrise. Mouth to minge beneath the ruined pier. Clichés of erotic desire. The yellow face of the sunflower climbing like Icarus into the warm currents of heliotropic myth. The raw and exposed wound of the Vietnamese girl scarred in eternity by the ejaculation of US desire.

The smile stops here. Marcel Duchamp added a moustache to the *Mona Lisa*, and a new name, *L.H.O.O.Q.* Pronounced in French this might translate as, 'She has a hot piece of tail!' Language is the hallucinogenic medium that destroys its creators in a thirst for exquisite configurations of meaning. Everything starts with an edit.

'So DS is Jewish and likes E. Am I missing something essential to the economy of this story?'

'No. Freud is Jewish. Marx is Jewish. My lover is Jewish. DS is serious product.'

'I think of her as a Rubic Cube. A twentieth-century toy and receptacle of love. A station for thought that has no home, an uncanny and difficult axis that baffles and delights us. DS is the extremity of parasitic design. She is space and consumes the phallus in its naming of things. She exhausts the rhetoric of love in the abyss of simulation.'

As culture became analogical I wanted to be anodyne, speak a sophormorphic dream in the ear of eternity. I have destroyed the breath that inflated the model. I am breathless and will abandon you on the scene of seduction. DS works the rhythm

to the bone and is submerged in other people's biophysics.
Like Warhol, she moves with the guiltless precision of a ghost.
Only her image remains.

Dave had just invited Sally into his office. He was excited
by the idea of interruption. A primal anxiety that manifests
itself in public exhibitions of lust. Dave de Fray was a lecturer
of English at Oxford. He was a born reactionary and lover
of Larkin. Sally, a visiting lecturer from Sussex, found his
ideas repulsive and feasted on his cock in masochistic delight.
He dribbled semen into her ass and she laughed.

DS and Julia leave Heaven together and catch a nightbus to
Battersea. On Lambeth Bridge the moon bleeds luminous blues
across a crash. An ambulance arrives to the sound of Jolly
Roger's *Acid Man.*

Coda Cipher

As she slept she had a dream. (You notice that even thinking
about Mark's arrival makes me call her Dolly.) The book had
grown fangs and had bitten her thigh. In her dream she was
made of flesh and blood. This incision not only made her
bleed but also aroused her. She wanted the fangs to stop teasing
her and suck her love muscle. The fangs were after blood not
vaginal fluids. DS was not alone in this fantasy.

There was a man with a case watching her. The case is on his
lap. It is an old case of beaten beige leather with frayed stitching.
Below the silver clasp are two neatly stamped letters in blood-
red Times Gothic: SF.

I rubbed my fingers in basil to remove the smell of garlic.
I threw the mixture into the oil.

'Why SF?' I asked myself.

Before I had the chance to rinse the pasta he was at the door
and giving the bell a familiar finger. It was ages since we had
seen each other. That strange mystery between two points
held us apart. Mark and Mark.

I opened the door and let him in. A pantomime of graces. He
watched as I ate and talked about Voltaire. After eating I offered
him a coffee. He loved coffee far more than Enlightenment
philosophers. We retired to the living room and talked. Then
we watched some TV. A programme called *The Big E* came
on and I started slagging off the people who had cashed in on
the acid house craze.

Her eyes closed. The book nestled on her breast. Her dreams
are my theoretical stratagems. We flap our wings to become
dancers and sink needles into her. The blood is removed
with somnambulistic cool. We inject each other with her virus.
Death rushes into our anaemic figures. Our veins dilate to
the size of scaffold tubes. Her tongue swims on warm currents.
Her mouth is a red velvet cave. She's kissing death. Death's
tongue is a silver train, twelve coaches long.

A bruised smile. Lipstick smudged over broken capillaries.
Opium dreams and alchemical diagrams. The infant Leonardo
gurgles in the dreams of Sigmund Freud. I wanted to stop,
rip open the seal and watch the cursor eat his words. The jaws
of a labyrinthodon should entice his paragraphs to the depths
and oblivion.

I thought of Leonardo sketching executions. Exiled from
Florence he sat like an assassin training his eyes on their target.
The face contorting, muscles in spasm, a mime drowned
in details of the period costume. His hand guided by the
knowledge of a mercenary in the era of Machiavelli.

Murder has been called a passionate art form. This is because
art evolved from magical hunting practices. The image fixes the
object in the mind of the hunter. Mammoth or man, each is
threatened by extinction as its coordinates are codified. Mark
slept with his shadow. I pulled the disc from the computer and
switched it off. I looked at the disc. How different it is to a book.
Where mythology and history were separated by marginal
horizons the world is now a system of digital mnemonics.

Between zero and one a smile broke across my face. I was
too busy to hustle the publishers. I would give my book
to Mark and let him re-write the novel one last time. I opened
the box that held my discs and picked out one with a label
of red insulating tape. I had picked up the habit of customising
my discs from Mark.

The standard CF2 was not a cool item. Mark always used blue
tape to mark his discs. I swapped the tape and deftly slipped
his disc into my box and left his on the table. When he opened
the file he would recognise the tone of my writing. He would
know that I had switched the discs. He would also know that
I had stolen his original version. If like me he had made a copy
he would be able to laugh.

I took a small wrap of coke from my wallet and lined up two
neat lines on the table beside the disc. Unlike psychoanalysis,
cocaine was a luxury I indulged in. Just this once I would share
it with Mark.

'Oi. Want a bit of Charlie?' I said rather loudly.

His head jerked back and his eyes opened wide. I passed him a note and gurned.

'Very sexy crystals!', he said, after sucking the line past the Queen's lips.

'Choo Choo', I said, and cleared the line.

Psychoscopia

Mark arrived at Brighton station at midnight. Still buzzing on the coke, he headed for the Zap. He followed the route of a thousand daytrippers. Down Queens Road, past the Victoria and Albert Clock, down West Street and its arcades to the seafront. He arrived there to find a small group of people waiting to get in. The club was small with a capacity of two hundred and fifty. Mark used to work on the door so he didn't have to wait. He was hustled past the group of leery lads trying to blag it. Inside, the club was rammed with a coach load of shoomers.

'All right matey?' said some geezer in a bandana and blue dungarees, face, neck and shoulders gleaming with sweat.

He held out a bottle of poppers. Mark declined and moved into the dark cavern. Strobes and smoke created curtains of imminent light.

'You viced up Marky?', said Nick before pulling some zombie moves on a pretty girl.

Mark saw a few more familiar faces dancing but the majority were lodgers, showing Brighton how to party. The bass thudded and the top end fragmented into wobbly Moog waves. Mark saw Anna through the smoke and moved towards her. People smiled and let him past. Anna was pissed and had brought two of her older students with her. The three Italians looked slightly dazed. English language books were full of photos of Teds, skins and punks, but this scene was something else.

Acid house had taken over where rare groove had met M.A.R.R.S. As rock 'n' roll had been launched on post-war affluence and Brylcreem, acid house found its niche in the Wall Street crash and the surplus wad from digitalising the international market. It was a wake for Thatcherism. A fusion of psychotropic soundscapes and a relapse into 1960s-style hedonism. It wasn't in the tourist guides of 1988 but it soon would be. Britain had long since stopped producing anything except hi-tech weapons systems and dodgy cults.

'Do you want a drink?', Mark shouted over the music.

'No thank you Mark. I'm pissed already!', Anna replied.

'Are you on one?', Sean asked at the bar.

'Fuck off! Not tonight mate, I'm with Charlie. Sort us out a Lucozade!', Mark shot back.

Mark returned to find that Anna had gone to the ladies. The two students were trying to master the quirky movements that the other dancers were doing. Hands waving like tentacles in warm inky sounds. They were smiling deliriously. Mark tranced out on the vibe and didn't notice Anna return. She was laughing and pulled his ear towards her mouth.

'Is Boy George here?', she asked.

Before Mark had time to think whether it was likely or not he walked past them looking wrecked and wearing the dressed down kit of the other shoomers. With this visual affirmation logged he replied.

'Yeah. Look, see for yourself!'

'Is it him? Is it Boy George?'

An ethereal voice filled the room. The melody phased and panned around the club. Hands reached up high. 'Reality, knowledge, feeling, truth. Reality, knowledge, feeling', then the voice sighed long and sensually and the rhythm kicked in. The dancers moved the current through a circuit. Zombies hiding from the cadaverous fears of the living, they let themselves become part of a network, a series of intensities that were contagious, seductive, deadly. They were the nightmare of E, radioactive souls emitting pure equations.

'Mark, he fell into the toilet with me. I was sitting there and he fell in with me. And then guess what he said?', Anna asked earnestly but she was obviously ready with the answer. Mark raised an eyebrow and Anna filled in the space.

'"What do you think of orgasms?", he said, "What do you think of orgasms?" And I said, "I love them!"' Anna was very excited.

By the end of the night everyone was dancing. DJ Faggot had moved seamlessly from Phuture into *The Promised Land* and everyone dripped with sweat as he worked two copies.

With all the house lights up and the party still kicking it could have gone on forever. Eventually he faded the record out and raised his hands in the air in a champion salute.

Mark made arrangements to meet Anna the next day to translate some sections of *Come* into Italian and left the club. Remarkably Anna turned up on time. It was a sunny Saturday afternoon and Mark felt pretty good. The raptures of acid house hadn't damaged Anna either, although she did confess that she hadn't scored. Anna seemed relaxed and sat down while Mark got a printout of the voice-over for her.

She began reading (sur)names. Multiple frames roll. The vertical hold is going. Alternatively the screen splits open, smearing the canvas of Leonardo da Vinci with the excrement of Antonin Artaud. These two image makers, these serial effects of technology. In the background the television relays football from the World Cup. The film rushes like a train across Tokyo. The final edit is never realised. The police say that Pasolini was beaten to death by a bit of rough. Before his death there was a rumour that Pasolini was working on the sex life of Leonardo da Vinci.

I situate us in the perfect theatre of her smile. We have no names, no faces, no story of our own. Clothes come off as the referee blows the final whistle. We fuck with the commentators discussing play. Between the beautiful and the sublime is the scrambled text of *Come*. I am the mannequin and model upon whom this smile descends. The hidden truth that sucks you into the whirlpool of words that bubble up from the breathing apparatus.

In my mother tongue she whispers: 'Seduction is my destiny.'

'What is this about?', Anna asked.

'Defacing art?', Mark replied enigmatically. Then, after pausing and looking at Anna he realised that she really was perplexed. Perhaps she was not into defacing art. 'It's about tripping. Acid and its effects on perspective. You can buy trips on blotting paper. Paper is impregnated with LSD. This is invisible to the naked eye but every trip has an image on it. This helps you cut it up and consume a safe dose. The images are iconic: Gorbachev, Superman, OHM, Yin and Yang, Strawberries, all sorts. The other day at Spectrum I bought a tab with the *Mona Lisa* on it and it blew me away. The illicit complicity between drug culture and art, alchemy and reality all fusing in this tiny bit of paper. The icon became symbolic of the synthesis of art and science. In the Louvre the *Mona Lisa* is trapped behind glass. Tourists end up photographing themselves. In the 1960s there were these badges that read, SUPPORT YOUR LOCAL TRAVEL AGENT—TRIP ON LSD.'

Mark looked at Anna for a response. She laughed and turned her eyes to the floor. For an hour she sat and worked through the writing. Every so often she stopped and asked Mark about the context and conjugation of adjectives and tenses. It was difficult writing to translate. Mark knew no Italian and everything she said sounded wonderful to him.

He loved her Lambretta accent. The way she revved her r's and reversed into the vowels. To him it sounded fantastic. When she had translated it, Mark set up the tape recorder and set the levels. Anna shuffled the pages and scribbled in corrections. When everything was ready Mark rolled a spliff to chill her out and let her relax into the reading. When she heard the results she was delighted.

When she had gone Mark listened to the tape again. A few sentences he recognised as his, but mostly it seemed as though she had given him a gift. Even if his ideas made no sense to people they would be able to relate to her voice. It drew you into a perspective and let you travel in its virtual dimensions. The voice, like the trace of writing, catches on invisible forests below the surface.

When Mark was six he fell into the sea and nearly drowned. He went under the water several times, screaming every time he surfaced. He called to his mother who was on the beach near the slipway. When he called the salt water punctuated his sentence. It was hardly a sentence. He was drowning, not waving. His mother was pregnant with his brother.

To rescue him she risked a miscarriage. She was furious with him. She pulled him out of the water and dragged him home. He was crying. Watching the red dye of her dress running down her legs his mouth was filled with the taste of salty burps. Recalling the vulture descending on Leonardo's cradle, this event was the realisation of his own mortality. The umbilical cord severed. The world was a sublime system of shocks. Some pleasurable, others terrible.

This event also marked him as a deadly shadow on the horizon of the 1960s, a flower child swimming into the psycho-tropical future. Academics have discovered that Freud's autobiography of Leonardo is a fantasy. Many of its founding details are located in errors. The vulture was probably a kite.

Home is not where the heart is but where time begins and the tunnel ends. Home is a memory that lights up inside; it draws you out of life into death. Where the Red Sea closed

our history began. Between the body and the wave we ride
on a layer of synthetic foam. Leonardo could have designed
surfboards as he spent hours watching waves and drawing
their form. Freud discovered that Lou Salomé had more than
a lush pussy. Together they consumed huge amounts of quality
cocaine and wrote long lists of names for the sexual organs.

Mark's smile is safe. Its placeless perfection seduces us as
it travels between the *Virgin on the Rocks, John the Baptist*
and the *Mona Lisa.* Like dancers who become possessed
by the beat, tourists gaze at the *Mona Lisa.* We are lost in
the euphoric smile and its obscure chemistry. Salomé (whose
silky underwear so seduced Freud) calls for the head of John
the Baptist. Her smile is the brilliant smile of forgetfulness,
the joy of losing oneself in the addictions of others. She
whispers to us in a language that is powerful and erotic.

In the daytime Mark would put on his hat and tails and
pose for the tourists. Standing absolutely still he became
the antithesis of a frantic dancer. Mark is a forename name.
It is also a verb. Between several marks and remarks are
words that will burn through the hemp…

Ltd Disco 45

Zealots rock to the Todd Terry groove. The Ministry of Sound's
custom built JBL system is pumping out repetitive beats. The
Friday night crowd is going bonkers. Security is mincing about
in official jackets. Wide yellow smiles contort out of frame.
Ecstasy enemas are delivered with complimentary tongue kung
poo. Speed is licked from magazine wraps. Water is expensive
and everyone wants it. Mark is one of the masses and craves its
simple formula.

The needle sits in the groove. A diamond tip tracing the spiral of information and passing it down the arm and into the mixing desk. Cryptic samples from TV and film, fragile bridges from reality. LA burns in video scratched symphonies. Older clubbers are thrown to the edge, bpms rise. Mark cruises the peripheries for eye food.

DS is an illicit product of the 1960s. Mark's father was Brian Jones. He fucked Mark's mother on a flight to LA. Jones died when Mark was five years old. Narcissus drowned in his own swimming pool reflection. He died to save us all. Like Jesus he dived into the abyss. Forty days in the psychedelic desert forever.

Cocteau said of himself, 'I am the lie that speaks the truth'. But he could have been talking about Brian Jones or his illegitimate son Mark. In Cocteau's version of *Orpheus* the mirror is a pool and cinema a version of mythology. Poems are blank sheets of paper. Modernity is a world upside down.

The DJ has a boxful of dodgy porno discs. This is the age of DS or artificial codes and layers of skin. This is the depth at which appearances become fatal and language is destroyed. I will sell DS to the highest bidder. It is fuck fiction.

By the time I left the Ministry I am wearing my rubber fuck fantasy. Words blanked out the holes in our imaginations and guided us in our orgasmic trajectory. That night I left alone. My indifference to sex was amplified by the quality drugs. Pornography suspends its economy until you want more and then you remember that every vice has a price. Two beautiful girls ambushed me on the steps of my flat.

'You got a light geezer?' I found a light before I found my keys.

I held out the lighter and the black girl leaned forward. She smiled and took a drag on a spliff and blew the smoke at me. She smiled again. A psychopathic smile that was troubling and subversive. The smile of a black planet or solar anus.

The white girl says, 'I'm Cozy, want some?'

She opened her coat. My pupils expanded by the rush of nubile flesh: she was naked except for a big pair of Caterpillar boots.

'What happened to your kit?'

'I swapped it for some drugs!' she said and pulled her hand out of her coat pocket and displayed a small plastic bag. Her flesh is creamy white and her pink pussy matched her needle-tipped breasts. She has a tasty scar just below her rib cage. It's weeping slightly.

'How did that happen?', I ask.

'Sfax and I were playing truth or dare.'

'Can Cozy and I come inside?'

'Do...'

'Cozy likes fucking strangers', Sfax says, closing the door behind her. Over her shoulder she has a black bag. She pulls out a camera.

'Do you want to star in a video fuck?', she asks casually.

'Are you serious?'

Cozy smiles and walks over to me. She takes hold of my belt and leads me towards my bed. She strips me. I open the wrap Mark and I had bought earlier.

'Can we?'

'Why not?', I reply.

She dips a wet finger into the coke and holds it out for Sfax. Sfax shakes her head. Cozy traces her wound with the powder. Climbing on top of me she lowers the wound to my mouth. I follow the crack in her flesh along the bitter trail of coke. She then puts her finger in again and circles my throbbing cock with Freud's aphrodisiac. She goes down on me sucking the drug like candles from a cake. Exquisite and silent choreography of sexual technique. I am out of my depth. Sfax hands Cozy a Durex. She pulls the rubber down my prick and terrifies me with her deft finger work and soaking pussy. It feels as if she's been fucking all night.

The vibrator: a sex machine with a secret history. A velocipede of transformative technology. The electric phallus is not a cock. Like the barrel of a gun it substitutes and defers the other tool in a transference matrix.

I'm stiff inside her. The succubine adoration of scars continues. This time I drop cocaine into the wound. This stings her. Her cunt clutches me. I lower my head to the wound in her flesh.

A zig-zag signature below her left breast. Sfax has a vibrator. My tongue searches for the coke that hasn't dissolved into her blood. Tiny crystals like boulders on the periphery of a volcano. Like the nasal cavity or the vaginal membrane, the wound provides the drug with routes into the blood system. Cozy licks the wrap clean and drops it.

Unlike Cozy, Sfax remains straight and clothed. Her dress is a web of cream lace. Her nipples and shaven Barbu, exquisite gifts of pornographic allure. Treasures adrift above her thigh-high boots. I fuck her friend; she practises her editing technique and direction skills.

'Come Mark, don't be shy, dish the cream!', she whispers softly.

Her face is partly obscured behind the camera. Shooting an overhead shot, flesh tracks, wet interludes.

'How many fucks have you got on tape?', I ask the camera.

Sfax smiles at me. It is a codified smile frozen in blood. The smile of the *Mona Lisa,* or Anti-Climax. A smile that is a rush of violence suppressed to realise a stratagem. I thought of the Brazilian tapes, soft porn subtexts of personal politics, erotic molotovs that bypass the censorship of morality. Cozy turned around on me. Her buttocks dripping with molten entropic desire. Sfax jumped over the bed. A chocolate alpine abyss of exposed vulva propelled on espresso thighs, scenic hallucination of black power, her lens draining the venery code that registered on my retina. My finger slides into Cozy. She rubs my testicles in the entropic ooze, her fingertips threatening castration. I envisage razor blades and plastic dope bags.

I feel fucked. Stereoscopic soundscape of the phuture, bass and kick drum cropped blonde head moving to and fro. I place my hands around her waist and then raise them.

Her ribs feel like the stolen wings of steel dinosaurs. She breathes like a monster from the prehistoric night. I have never had sex with a stranger before. This is a fantasy timed within the horizon of pre-viral sexuality. I see the golden Durex disappear, a surgical perversion and realisation of infantile research. I am Mr Y and she is an insane victim of self-laceration. In her cunt I find the *Tropic of Capricorn*.

Sfax pans up like an insect. The prosthetic eye zooming in on the crimson vacuity of Cozy's mouth, white teeth and pastel pink tongue. Sfax has the vibrator in her hand. She moves around to my right and lets it buzz in my ear. An auditory diversion from her perverse proximity and distance. I close my eyes and almost simultaneously feel the metal head against my lips. She parts my lips with the device and I don't resist. The machine is buzzing in my mouth. I am the centre of a cybererotic fusion of circuit-chic…

I am the powerless star of Sfax's white skin trade epic, *White Boys Suck.* I open my eyes. I am sucking on the vibrator. Sfax winks at me. Cozy lifts herself off my cock. Turning around she takes the vibrator from my lips and runs it along the wound. My barrel is ready to unload into the Durex Gold. She takes hold of it and flexes it gently in her hand. With the other hand she runs the vibrator across my sperm sacks and slowly down towards my anus.

It is someone else's story. She slowly eases it into the solar anus and then takes her throne upon my cock. The wound is raw and still seeping its translucent blood. In mutual spasms of pleasure and pain we work quickly with pseudo-military efficiency towards orgasm. Sfax takes all the shots. A rapid succession of angles, spunky geometry of pubis and obsolete ruses of arousal. Pharmatropic propaganda for a perverse

polysexuality. Cozy gets up and her ass looks red. Her boots
cool. Sfax follows her as if she was prowling a catwalk, a super
feline model of nihilistic fecundity. I was the ecstatic prop.
Infant penis sleeping on my stomach. They walk across
my room and Sfax follows Cozy out into the night in search
of the next fifteen-minute star. I wished I'd had a camera or
they'd invite me along. I never saw them again.

Deep Dream Remix

Between a show on tantric sex and a story that became
incomprehensible, I found myself speculating on placement
advertising in literature. Was *American Pyscho* literature,
or carnivorous sales talk?

I watch as a machine tests a pink Durex. There is a woman's
voice. Then there is a woman. Like DS she speaks and
I mediate, a mercenary in the field of information. She
hums pop songs to herself as she works. She operates the
condom conveyer belt in a prophylactic factory. The factory
is busy because as we all know there is a boom in the market.
The technology seems primitive. The economy is lubricated
by tongues. The factory system, like sex, seems destined
to become a nostalgic memory. Like science fiction, sex will
change its name to stay hip.

DS is produced in a factory similar to the one in which
the condoms are made. She is non-perishable and reusable.
Flesh participates in sex. DS is troubled. She is a model like
other models, serial number PZ092. She is a commodity
that is packaged and distributed according to the value of
the product.

Her box was like all the others. Destined for Japan via an ad in *Flash*, she recalls the cute picture of her inflatable bimbo profile. The bimbo text in pastel pink symbols. The value of the product had risen while she was sitting on the shelf. Japan was faddish. After nipple clamps had come transparent dildos, pot noodles and then...WOW! Three price rises in a month. A whole lotta yen.

DS was heading for the States. Bought by a Californian who collected erotic memorabilia. Inside her packaging she was like any other doll. He could have bought her in San Fransico for half the price. But he liked the packaging. He was a New Age Pervy King who knew how to impress his freaks. He didn't keep her in the box of course. He used her. He even customised her. DS was revamped to look very hardcore. That was how she got her first film part.

A friend of the Pervy King used to rib him about how obsessed he was with his inflatable spunk trap. Then this other freak came up with the idea of using her in a film with Dennis Hopper. The Pervy King was jealous but he loved Hopper.

The celebrity train wreck was cast as a fucked-up dealer with a psychotic fixation on this inflatable doll. Dolly got to hang with Hopper. He would fuck her at parties, whisper to her between shoots. It was a dream-like period. The film went on to be a cult smash. Crispin Glover in particular ravished the lexicon of amphetamine babble.

DS was not nominated for an Oscar. But what the fuck! Neither was Hopper. He was fantastic. The most touching moment in the movie was when Hopper prevents the killer from molesting DS and screams as he hugs her, 'I ain't no fuckin' psycho—I know she's a doll!'

She got another film role immediately afterwards and the Pervy King didn't stand in her way. It was a low budget art house movie. It was sensual in a dumb way. DS had a bit part in a porn store. It was a rather blunt flashback to her origins without the exoticism. She was just dragged out of a drawer in a New York store, soft and deflated.

DS began to crave a place in someone's fantasies. And it was at this point that our paths crossed. I was researching *An Illustrated History of Sexual Paraphernalia* and had been given the Pervy King's address by some friends in Brighton. I got out to New York on a Hoover ticket and decided to check him out. I spent a week there. Every day I would call with my camera and shoot a couple of rolls of film, discuss the prints from the day before and record conversations with the Pervy King. His knowledge was truly encyclopaedic. To cut a long and seedy story short, he gave her to me. Then she was launched into the narrative of *Come.*

In this story her lover betrays her. DS was terminated with multiple wounds to her body. In the dead of night, two laughing women tossed her into a bin. In the morning she was thrown in with other plastics destined for recycling. With thousands of Volvic bottles her last cognisant moment was on a conveyor belt heading for reincarnation.

1. EXTERIOR. BRIDGE. NIGHT.
A body floats into frame and under a bridge. It is an inflatable doll covered in body paint. In her mouth is a speaker. Her face fills the screen. The speaker emits an eerie recording of a woman's voice, 'You can't fuck with me.' The screen goes black.

2. INTERIOR. BEDSIT. NIGHT.

A macro shot of a keyboard and a man typing in the letters,
C.O.M.E, this is ANTI-CLIMAX. The camera pulls out
to show him at a table with an open book and a computer.
The camera takes frantic close-ups of his face and then pauses.
The camera pans around to his ear and the image breaks up.
In the disrupted frame we see a woman, SEX, on a leather
couch wearing a set of 1970s headphones.

3. EXTERIOR. BRIGHTON. SUMMER DAY.

A spinning air vent. MAX walks past the spiral blades and is
followed by a low scanning camera. He makes his way past the
Grand Hotel, through the subway and onto Brighton beach.
Among the old pillars of the West Pier he reads into a cassette
recorder. With his fingers he gently spins the water in a rusted
iron socket that used to support the original superstructure
of the pier.

4. INTERIOR. BEDSIT. NIGHT.

We cut to SEX, who is again on the couch, wearing headphones
and lying face down in a t-shirt emblazoned with the message,
Blow my Mind!

5. INTERIOR. LOUNGE. NIGHT.

From MAX's point of view we see SEX stretch and grab
something from the concrete floor and hurl it towards him.
It is a soft globe used by money traders to release stress.
It impacts with a playful thump on the glass.

SEX: What do you want?

MAX: I've got some software for you.

SEX: Yeah ok! I'll come when...I'm ready.

6. INTERIOR. BEDSIT. NIGHT.

MAX is in a silent orange room. He is busy laying out red
material next to an orange and a plastic bag on a silver sofa.
SEX enters and sits down in front of MAX. We see that her
t-shirt has an inflatable doll's head on the front with a gun
sight centred on it.

MAX: Shall I read to you?

SEX: No don't bother, I'll listen to the tape.

As if this were a command, MAX picks up a Walkman and
a set of headphones and passes them to SEX who is winding
on a throwaway camera. He stands stiffly in front of her.

MAX presses play as SEX ties him to the silver sofa. His
voice fills her ears. She pauses between knots to photograph
his bound body. Hitching up her skirt SEX climbs onto him.
MAX smiles in complicity and raises his head to let her insert
an orange into his mouth. SEX uses her fingers to bruise his
windpipe and his eyes bulge.

Necroticism

I pick up the phone and dial 01273_____ Mark is out. I wait
for the tone and leave this message, 'I am telling you a story.
I am a ventriloquist. A preacher of addiction. My act goes like
this. It's a memory trick. You have lost the plot!'

Wanting to numb out I switch on the TV, attaching myself
to the abandoned terminus of the metropolis. I channel hop.
White noise pulsing between random scenes. Dr X, or
Stentorphone as he is sometimes called, caught a tube

to the university. As he read the adverts he realised he had left his notes at home, in his handbag. He was a TV and often came to the university in drag but today he hadn't had time to do himself up. He had to give a lecture, bpm, Beyond Postmodernism.

DS inhales the scenario, her body deflating between ideas, in empathy with his rhythm and the swaying tube. Dr X entered the lecture theatre like an assassin. Obsessed with the termination of his subjects.

'Hello', he said, warning them. 'I am mourning under the slightly heady epitaph, bpm. There will be no preamble to this lecture because I have forgotten my notes, however the tonality of my address should become miraculously clear.'

As the familiar drone of a lecture starts, various students slouch forward onto their notebooks, the theatre lights go down. 'I want to start by quoting Avital Ronell.'

DS reads Stentorphone as a code propelled into the inflatable dimension of her subjectivity. She speculates on her addictions. Her love for novels. Her ability to fold her pages in an anachronistic fashion and believe in herself as any other body without organs might do.

Let your eyes breathe in the romance of perspective. The red lips of Tess swallowing the strawberry. Imagine the unmapped territory of her oesophagus. The sky is a piece of blotting paper with ink spilling through it, staining it, as in Hardy's *Tess.* Or is it the pharmakon that flows into the story through the process of printing. The letters SF are illuminated signs of another discourse. Let your eyes breathe in the romance of perspective. The red lips of Tess swallowing the strawberry. Imagine the unmapped territory of her oesophagus.

'The biodynamics of her consumption are like mine. Her interior is full of fecundity, trapped and decomposing like a serial killer's shrine. My story begins normally enough. Once upon a time there was a factory — it made inflatable dolls. These were produced to suit every taste, from *Baywatch* inflatables like Tara, with her suntan, sensitive mouth and inviting vagina, for merely $30 to Cleopatra, whose price of $544 was due to the infinite list of her intensive features including, movable limbs, real human hair, battery powered vibrating vagina, firm breasts that lactate, juice gland...(for when she gets over-excited) and a plethora of special effects that define excitation, for the sophisticated user. I was made in Hong Kong. My original name was Eko.'

Mark wakes up to the assaulting tone of breakfast TV. The hosts are recoiling in horror. Colin Wilson is waxing lyrical about the *Dracula* meets the *Bride of Frankenstein* dynamic of Fred and Rosemary West's relationship. They don't know how to end the interview or respond to his lighthearted résumé of their blood orgy. The mood shifts abruptly as they announce the next item following the death of another teenager on E. TV is fucked. New York is fucked. Tokyo is fucked. London is fucked.

Vogue

DS is an amplification of a signal, a fetish submerged in the everyday. Transparent stimulant, her voice is sexual. She is an actress. Her sexuality moulds itself to your desires. She turns you on and silently inflates the impotency of the model. Lines discontinued, empty houses, cars with radio's stolen, these are the ruins that delight her, vague spaces where she can let you play with her. DS. Not even a proper name, not

even a doll. A snub-nosed noise of addictive dissemination.
She is a flipside. A B-side.

Cocteau is on opium. In a reverie his friend Apollinaire
is telling the story of how Picabia stole the *Mona Lisa*.
The fingerprints were everywhere. A series of stories about
Leonardo da Vinci. Leonardo invents an erotic automaton
for a wealthy patron. It was a beautiful model called *Mona*.
Her sexual organs were particularly well-crafted and deviated
from the line drawings on which Freud based his infamous
repulsion theory.

The Da Vinci necrophile file: page upon page of notes
and translations from Latin into Italian on the court case
of Gilles de Rais. Leonardo had become obsessed after
finding a signature in the front of a richly bound copy of
Metamorphosis, received in payment for a brothel design
in 1497. A text on the strategic effect of biochemical
experiments by Leonardo during his commission as a military
technician. Barely recognisable atomic patterns, developed
by Leonardo from the black death virus, hide a horrific tale.

The plastic began to age. DS is caught at bad angles. Naked,
her nipples are semi-erased. In the intimate spaces marked
by the absence of Marks, her words search like lips in the
dark…for someone to seduce. Other tunes are being mixed
down for the long summer rush. Someone let the mood
fuck up real bad. DS is in the house. Freaky dancer. Drug
head. Dreamer. TV guest.

Animated like an Arabian knight, her particles drift in
nomadic trails across an illusionary horizon. She is a mirage
of masked desire dismembered for articulating without
compromise, a different chronological perspective. She partied

on the high vibe while governments supplied arms designed by psychopathic technophiles. It's cool.

Between the CJA and MDMA, life is an equation in ruins, a culture of the artefactual debris of history. Time is the soapy abyss through which her body is floated. Cum is erased from her mouth. She speaks a clean language of cunt/cock aphrodisiacs, a mind-fucking nutrient that dissolves with acidic appetite the story and its cartography.

Sfax and Cozy add voice-overs and leftover dub vibes. The tapes are sold to hip magazines and decadent emporia of PVC sleaze. Cozy and Sfax modified DS with crude sensor pads. Engulfed in her, they began to play in the dimension of their body space. Tripping and colliding, their bodies merge in sensory pleasures. Mutually accommodating electrical storms, they feed each other's wired impulses to the max. The sound of double breathing signifies the proximity of virtual orgasm. Sex is a virtual lay-line to the unconscious.

DS is transformed by the technical vectors that encode her. Cozy had found her on a shelf with Zara and Adam. Perhaps DS was trying to get some more info on UK models. Adam was modelled on Jeff Stryker. He reclined on his ankles to display his stiff sixty degrees. He was handled by both sexes. A libertine adept she is used like a toy to navigate playtime in the syntax of power, sex and the other commodities that Sfax and Cozy thrive on.

Beyond her ZERO/ONE interface DS becomes familiar with the figurative gestures of the feminine. Sfax and Cozy are oblivious to her fascination with the minute detail of their lives. As they work during the day, phoning distributors, art house cinemas, printers, festivals, and engage with all the tedium that is the flipside to their lucrative video-fuck business, they are scanned by her receptors. From her invisible position she would steal their easy sense of themselves. DS wants more than real hair, she needs an authentic aura. The visual resolution is not perfect, but better than a 1970s skinflick.

The curve of the smile is rolling between frames. The super-imposed negative is a dense tube. Mark is standing beside a tomb on which is laid a Xerox of the *Mona Lisa*. It is a Super-8 movie. No dialogue. Mark places flowers on the smiling face.

We read texts to lace the narrative with fragments of the pharmakon. Already the double mimes these 'TRUTHS' and erases the name DS. The paint is peeled away with sub-atomic precision and the perversity of the line is revealed. Its author a master of the Priory of Sion, spent hours hiding ciphers on the palms of her hands. She holds the key to the Temple of Solomon. John the Baptist is merely the guide.

She is dubbed into Italian. Do you remember these details, this mysterious web of sceneless stories, sugary soundscape and proliferation of zeros? An 'O' opens in the centre of space. It is a ring and orifice of the solar anus. The ZERO is infinite. Twice. It is repeated in the name 'Leonardo'. Flying around like cogs of subliminal desire. DS is an emerging icon and strap-on sensibility. A blank face with a catatonic smile.

Carbon 14

Mark meets Mona in Kensington Arcade. She has a handful of flyers. Without losing track of their conversation, she vibes the right punters and hands them select promo. Party people take the simulated drugs wraps with conspiratorial smiles.

'Yeah, Mark heard things are going well?'

'It's alright, Julia and I and met with Shinya's producer, Kiyo Joo.'

'Sounds exciting?'

'He really likes the idea but won't make it on anything smaller than eight million! We talked to the BFI and they're like, "So who are you? Could you do a kind of cyber-sleaze, sixty-grand thing?" And we're like…NO!'

Mark reads the small print, Mona works the crowd shuffling through the North Lanes; old skool cheesy quavers, trustafarians, stinkers, slackers, the cast of *Quadrophenia*, lager lasses, pig city skaters, no wave punks, jazzauls, animals, pierced primitives, dreaded teds, men from Hugo Boss, girls from Whitehawk, geezers from the City, shy boys in Fred Perry, flygirls from the night before…junglists in yer face 'cos you've lost the bass.

Mark moves off towards the Dorset. The street outside is crowded with phantoms from Glastonbury. All the accoutrements of slackerville are on sale. A few in shops, most of them falling out of trunks and scarves onto the street. Between a *Big Issue* seller and a *SchNEWS* reader, Mark finds a seat and lights up a fag.

Mark is waiting for Mark to come. The scenery gets moved about as some wannabe art director decides that real people are spoiling the street life scene. Mark's vigilant and soon clocks a Moschino dress falling from the shoulder of a model. The velvet dress is a deep indigo with silver embroidery texts.

Mark One becomes slightly agitated by the thought that Mark Two was probably just standing still in Pavilion Gardens. His mood improved when he began to speculate on the model's lingerie. What's she wearing? Is it cool to ask?

Moschino girl is bathing in the silent ineptitude of Mark's gaze. She is almost tempted to switch sides but the session isn't over yet.

Two weeks ago Mark saw Mark on TV with DS beside him. He was making her talk. You can see inside her. She has no womb, no rectum, no intestine, no aorta, liver or kidneys, she does not correspond to the maps of the body or the drawings of Leonardo. DS is a virtual cover girl, her inflamed pixels are a hot commodity. Dead or alive the flash fixes her gaze. Her mouth slightly open. Her eyes slightly shut. She is the dose of LSD in the dying body of Aldous Huxley. DS impregnates all her surfaces with the pharmakon.

Repulsion

DS arrives in Paris at 10.20am and takes a taxi from the airport. She even says a few words in French to the driver. Either her pronunciation was wrong or the driver wasn't into speculative monologue as a mode of small talk. He merely asked her for fifty francs as he pulled up by the metro.

'Merci', she said politely as he drove off. DS is lost between lovers. She reads the spray paint outside a Bastille gallery.

'Parisian graffiti is classy shit!', she thought to herself.

Inside the gallery hermaphrodites and transexuals were posed close to the lens. DS was far away from the original matrix of her identity. She had become expandable beyond all the limits of literature. Some might have called her the sublime dominatrix of the text.

At last the line clears. I select Mark's number and press send. At the other end the text will come without a header.

A limousine drives through Paris. In the back a group of bodies consume each other's excrement, giddy and fermented words tainted by their human tongues. DS, like Gilles de Rais, was not a pervert but a parasexual projection into the organs of the erotomechanic machine. The car glides across the Seine, transporting the headless joy riders deep into the networks of the city. As they pause for the lights a sea of silent people cruise past.

DS thinks that she has spotted Stentorphone or Dr X. He is sitting at a crossroads. He is wearing a smart black suede dress. He doesn't look his age at all. His face looks delicate in the evening light. She sits at a table close enough to eavesdrop. Dr X, 'La Pucelle continued to beat inside me. I tried to drive out this snake coiled up inside my back.'

DS is good at remembering conversation but she couldn't figure out the direction of their dialogue. She found herself ingesting semi-masticated pulp. DS is an undercover agent for SERIAL. She is sure that it is Stentorphone. As he departs she follows him, as always he loses her in the metro. She takes out her mobile and phones the embassy. She can't get a connection.

Disco 2000

The *Mona Lisa* has an oiled texture that masks the stubble of
the transvestite posing for tourists. Perhaps she inspired Oscar
Wilde to declare that nothing assumed in life is as seductive
as a pose. Femininity is the sacrificial pose of the erotic
code. Every superficial surface sacrifices itself to the pleasure
of penetration.

DS and her lover are travelling on the underground. The
tube is full. DS and her lover are suspended from handgrips.
Marshmallow cocks, unarticulated vocabularies, wait to
penetrate our sleeping ears. Erotomania erupts in the dark
soil beneath the City. Their bodies become inseparable,
melted like Siamese twins into a moist multiple invagination.
Agitated eyes drip salty sweat over the lens. Eyes zoom in
primitive excitement at the wet lips communicating.

Turning like an actress DS moved down Beak Street, forgetting
Breathless and her lover, she counted the numbers on the
doors. She arrived at no.30 slightly out of breath but on time.
Her destination was down a long corridor and past an open
yard. DS ringed the bell marked C Seance.

'Hello. Can I help you?', a voice asked.

'Yes, I've come for an appointment with Cherry Seance.'

'Who is this?', asked the voice.

'My friends call me DS.'

'Oh, Mark's friend. Come in.'

DS moved through the hallway. A door opened and a casually-dressed woman of thirty-five appeared. She reached out her hand and DS held it. It was soft, sophisticated; a manicured sensory interface.

'Hi, I'm Cherry. Come in.' she said, pointing into her office. DS walked into a room decorated with Victorian furniture. Cherry pointed at a chair.

'So what's the job?', asked DS.

'Well, Geovisual has been one of the foremost UK ad agencies. However we are now expanding into features. Channel 4 likes our style and have asked us to show them a pilot for a series.'

'What is the series about?', prompted DS.

'We have bought the rights to a novel about Gilles de Rais.'

Cherry got up and walked over to a bookshelf. She returned with a hardback and placed it on the table in front of DS. The cover was white and embossed with the word *Come.*

Bubble Entendre
Mark Waugh
Semina No. 3
Published and distributed by Book Works, London

ISBN 978 1 906012 12 0

Commissioning editor: Stewart Home
Edited by Stewart Home and Gavin Everall
Designed by Fraser Muggeridge studio
Printed by Die Keure, Bruges

Book Works
19 Holywell Row
London
EC2A 4JB
www.bookworks.org.uk
tel: +44 (0)20 7247 2203

Book Works is funded by Arts Council England